D0984400

Don't Look Behind You

Don't Look Behind You

Marilyn Ross

Five Star
Unity, Maine

LS MAO MC

Copyright © 1973 by Marilyn Ross

All rights reserved.

Five Star Romance.
Published in conjunction with Maureen Moran Agency.

Cover photograph © Alan J. La Vallee

April 1999
Standard Print Hardcover Edition.

Five Star Standard Print Romance Series.

The text of this edition is unabridged.

Set in 11 pt. Plantin.

Printed in the United States on permanent paper.

Library of Congress Catalog Card Number: 98-94840
ISBN: 0-7862-1810-X

To Bob Hoskins, editor and author

Chapter One

It had happened on a windy, rainswept night in October of 1968. Beth Lindsay knew she would always remember that stormy night with all its eerie details etched deeply on her mind. For one thing, it had been the night of the Moores' thirtieth anniversary and she had been a house guest of the millionaire mine owner and his family at the time. The great graystone mansion, which was one of the showplaces of Marblehead, faced the Atlantic from one of those rugged cliff sites so familiar along the stern Massachusetts coastline.

When she'd had her first glimpse of the rambling house with its impressive front steps and white columns flanking the broad front door of light oak, she'd had a feeling of uneasiness. This was strange, for there was no reason that she should have. At that moment she could not have guessed what the old mansion would mean to her or the ordeal of horror she would know within its formidable walls laced with colorless vines.

Of course she'd been ill at the time and just freshly arrived from Botswana in South Africa, where she'd been living with her father and where she'd met the Moores. When she'd been stricken with a bout of a rare tropical fever, the doctor with the company constructing the dam had suggested that she get away for awhile. He suggested the United States or some other more moderate climate.

"What about the Moores?" her distinguished-looking engineer father had suggested with a smile on his lean, tanned face. Frank Lindsay had moved from one construction job to another in outlandish corners of the world for years. And since the divorce which had robbed her of her mother, Beth had lived with him, apart from time spent at boarding schools and college until her graduation two years before.

She'd glanced up from the pillow of the company hospital bed with a shy smile on her high-checked, intelligent face. "I don't think I'd want to bother them," she protested mildly. A little on the tall side, she had grown into a lovely auburn-haired beauty with the large green eyes and slighty petulant lips of the mother she remembered only vaguely now.

"I'm sure it would be a pleasure for them," Frank Lindsay said. "I know they enjoyed your company here. We entertained them and they would like to return the hospitality. You've been hearing from them, haven't you?"

"Yes."

Her father had smiled at her and taken one of her hands in his. "It's time you got away from here and met some new people. And if I remember rightly, young Stan Moore seemed very interested in you."

She blushed. "You imagine things, Dad. We were just good friends. But I would like to see Helen again."

"That's the sister," her father recalled. "Nice girl. And I was impressed by the parents as well. For a man with a lot of money, Stephen Moore has a social conscience, and his wife is nice. You should get in touch with them."

"Perhaps I will," she said.

"Do," her father insisted. "You can spend a little time with your Aunt Grace in Bermuda and then take a plane to Boston. Since Marblehead is only a few miles from the city, the Moores could meet you there."

"I'll see," she said. "There's another son, Alex, who didn't come over here with them. I believe he works in Boston. At least he's a librarian at Harvard in Cambridge. Perhaps he could meet me."

"Don't worry about the details. Get better and write them."

And so as soon as she felt a little more like herself, she sent an airmail letter to Helen Moore, telling the American girl she would be in the United States shortly and would like to visit the family in Marblehead if it were convenient. In the days in which she waited for a reply, she recuperated on the screened veranda of her home in a new section of the Botswana capital of Gaberones.

Her father was one of a group of specialists working in the newly formed country to try and bring it more in step with the rest of the world. As a colonial area of France it had remained largely undeveloped. Now an independent nation, it was using loans from the United States and other countries to try and become self-supporting.

Water was one of the vital needs for farming and cattle raising. And so Frank Lindsay was associated with a company building several dams and canals to help the drought-ridden land. Beth had come to join him and at first had been shocked by the poverty and backward ways of the people. But now she was beginning to adjust and share their hopes.

Stephen Moore had flown to Africa to take a close look at his copper mining interests. Botswana had been included in his itinerary and he and his wife, along with his son and daughter, had stayed in Gaberones for nearly two weeks. It was during this period Beth and her father had gotten to know the millionaire and his family. Beth had been especially thrilled. She'd known so little of true family life, having only her father, that the Moores seemed an ideally happy group.

And despite her protests to her father, she had been particularly interested in dark-haired, serious Stan Moore. She and

9

the earnest young man from Marblehead had spent a lot of time in each other's company.

She clearly remembered one afternoon when they had driven in a jeep they borrowed from her father to a spot a distance from the dam to admire the looming heights of its concrete barriers. It was at this point a river was to be contained and its water divided to much of the arid land.

At the wheel she turned to him and smiled. "Now you can really see what we're doing?"

"I think it's great," the young man said enthusiastically. "And so does my father." His serious eyes met hers as he went on. "I'm also surprised to find that I had to travel all the way to this so-called dark continent to find a girl like you."

She arched an eyebrow. "And what's so special about me?"

"Well," he said, "aside from the fact you're pretty and I have a weakness for redheads, you're intelligent and concerned. You really care what happens to this country and these people."

"I do," she agreed. "I learned that from my father. He likes to believe in what he is doing."

Stan Moore nodded. "He's a fine man. What about your mother? I didn't like to ask him."

She sighed. "They were divorced years ago. She lives in England. She didn't approve of the rugged life and ran off with some friend of Dad's. I don't know all the details. I hardly remember her."

Stan Moore showed embarrassment. "I'm sorry. I shouldn't have asked you about that."

"I don't mind. It happened a long while ago," she said. There was a pause. "Of course, I won't say I haven't missed having a mother. I have. That's why I think you and your family are so lucky. A tightly knit family group is so wonderful."

Stan smiled wryly. "We can bother each other at times."

"That's to be expected," she said. "But you do have each other. I'm grateful for father but I often find my life lonely."

Stan gave her a meaningful look. "You'll soon be getting married and beginning a family of your own. I suppose there's a young man back in the States or somewhere who is waiting for you to join him."

"Wrong," she said.

Stan said, "You're not engaged?"

"No. Oh, I've had chances," she said quickly. "But perhaps I've not met the right man. And then, I don't like to leave father. I feel he would be quite alone without me, and with my schooling finished I can devote my entire time to him."

"You can't do that forever," the young man argued. "And you can't hide yourself in this jungle for years either. You're cheating yourself of the chance for a normal life."

She'd smiled patiently. "I'm afraid I don't see it that way. I enjoy being here and I feel I owe father a lot of loyalty to make up for what my mother did."

Stan had eyed her with concern. "That's actually the thing that rules you, isn't it? Your life is shadowed by what your mother did. You feel you have to sacrifice yourself because of her."

She shook her head. "It's not all that clearly defined in my mind."

"But I'd say that's what it amounts to," he told her. "If I had just a little longer here, I'd try to change your thinking. But we're leaving tomorrow. Come and see us in the States, Beth."

"I'll think about it."

"I'll not forget you," he'd promised. And to underline his promise, he'd taken her in his arms and held her. After some gentle kisses he let her go and they drove back to the town, happy for their moment shared.

The following day Beth and her father had accompanied the four members of the Moore family to the airstrip where their private plane awaited them. Standing before the great aluminum monster of the skies, Beth shook hands with the gray-haired, aristocratic Stephen Moore and with his middle-aged, fragile wife, Andrea. Then she said goodbye to brunette Helen and lastly to Stan. The dark, intense young man held her hand just a little longer than the others and his goodbye was more tinged with emotion.

She and her father stood watching until the large private plane had taken off and was on its way to Capetown. She gave a final wave standing there in the bright sunshine and her throat was tight and her eyes blurred with held-back tears. If her father noticed, he made no comment as he took her by the arm and headed back to their jeep.

Later, in the African night, she lay awake thinking about it all, especially how much she'd enjoyed the Moore family and perhaps even envied their mutual happiness. Again she realized what a lonely life she and her father led. But she had no wish to change it; not if it meant leaving him alone. And there was little likelihood of his ever marrying again. He seemed completely absorbed by his work.

Stan had wisely said that much of her life had been influenced by her mother's abandonment of her and her father those many years ago. She gazed up into the shadows of the mosquito net hung over her bed and tried to visualize her mother as she'd last seen her. Beth had been only a child and so her mother had seemed very tall and beautiful. And cold! Her kisses had always been brief and she'd had a habit of pushing Beth away from her quickly after a barely polite embrace.

Her manner had left Beth upset and desolate. And she remembered the tears she'd shed when her father had tried to gently break the news to her that her mother had gone away for a long visit. She had known it meant that she'd never see her mother again. And she hadn't in all the years since!

That night after the Moores' departure she suffered a familiar nightmare, one that had tormented her since she'd been a broken-hearted child in pigtails. It was a reenactment of her mother's kissing her a cool goodbye and leaving her for what would be forever. In the dream she always ran after her mother, followed the car down the dusty road sobbing out to her to return.

And after that the nightmare always became muddled. She ran this way and that fruitlessly trying to locate her missing mother and never finding her. Then she would hear her father's voice calling to her and try to locate him. But she couldn't! She was lost in a thick forest from which there was no escaping. She ran on and on until the earth seemed to open and swallow her up. She screamed as she twisted in torment and came awake dripping with perspiration.

Her scream frightened and shamed her. It was a little girl's nightmare which kept coming back to haunt her. She should have outgrown it long ago. But she hadn't! Somewhere deep in her subconscious the horror of losing her mother remained. The scar was too deep to be erased, even though she could rationally accept the nightmare for what it was!

The dark side of Africa had never troubled her until she was struck by the fever. Others in the camp had suffered the mysterious illness and one young engineer had died, while several emerged from weeks in sickbed looking emaciated and haunted. She'd been talking to the black woman who acted as their housekeeper about the evening meal when suddenly the room had begun to swirl around her and she collapsed.

After that she experienced a series of wild, tormenting fever dreams. She had lain ill for long days and nights without even being aware of the passage of time. Then had come brief lapses when her mind was clear enough to recognize that she was in a room of the company hospital with either her father or their housekeeper by her bed. But the feverish nightmares kept returning; dreams of violence and terror in which she and her father were attacked by faceless enemies, or in which she saw some horrible crime being enacted before her terrified eyes.

At last the nightmares began to fade and the periods when she was conscious lengthened. She came to recognize the doctors and nurses who attended her and she felt secure when her father visited and sat with her.

The housekeeper also came to break the lonely hours in the hot hospital room. The old woman's wizened black face gazed down at her with pity and she murmured words which Beth could not fully understand.

"The cursed sickness," the old woman said softly. "That is what you have! Someone hates you and had the witch doctor strike you down this way!"

She'd looked up into the concerned black face with troubled eyes and protested, "No. It's just some sort of fever!"

"I know the fever!" the housekeeper said grimly. "It is the voodoo! You will never be free of it! The curse will follow you!"

Beth had tried to close her mind to the superstitious talk of the ignorant old woman. But she knew this was Africa with its strange ways and she wondered. She spoke to her father about it and he was angry and scornful about what the old woman had said.

14

"Native superstition!" he scoffed. "Don't even give it a second thought."

She'd tried not to. But it was hard to forget, the old woman had seemed so sincerely concerned. Then her father had suggested her visiting Bermuda and America and she'd turned her mind to the trip. Within a short while she had a warm reply from Helen Moore. The gist of it was that they'd be delighted to see her and have her stay with them as a house guest for as long as she liked. Nothing much had changed, Helen had confided, except that she'd become engaged and Stan was married.

Stan was married! This news had been a blow to Beth. She'd been looking forward to seeing the serious and rather handsome young man again. Perhaps she'd even had hopes of some romance between them. But then she'd given him little encouragement with her talk of always remaining with her father. If he had forgotten her, or simply written her off as a possible wife, she had only herself to blame.

Her desolation almost made her give up the idea of the trip. But her doctor gave her little choice. He insisted she must get away from Africa for awhile if she were to recover. So her father took her down to Capetown, helped her shop for a new wardrobe, and saw her off on the first leg of her plane journey to Bermuda and New England.

The holiday with Aunt Grace in Bermuda proved pleasant but rather boring. Her aunt lived alone and had few young friends, so Beth found herself almost continually in the company of old people. She was relieved when the time came to take the plane to Boston. She'd had a letter from Helen and in it Helen had said that her brother Alex would be meeting Beth at Logan Airport.

Beth arrived at the Boston airport after the short two-hour

flight from Bermuda. She was wearing one of her smartest travel outfits, a rose knit dress and matching coat. She searched the faces of the waiting people who had come to greet the plane and saw none that resembled the Moores.

When she'd about despaired of having anyone meet her, a slender, thin-faced young man with horn-rimmed glasses emerged from the waiting crowd to ask her, "Are you Beth Lindsay?"

"Yes, I am," she'd replied delightedly, taking in the rumpled brown tweeds and unkempt hair of the young man and deciding that he had to be Alex, the academic member of the Moore family.

"I'm Alex," he said, making her compliment herself on her perception. "What about your bags?"

She turned with a rueful smile. "I expect they are on that revolving thing."

"One of the worst hazards of flying is reclaiming luggage," Alex Moore said grimly. "If you'll point them out to me, I'll at least make an attempt to retrieve them."

"Thank you," she said and moved closer to the revolving luggage carrier which was surrounded by a lot of nervous, complaining, grasping people. She pointed out her two bags and Alex got them on the first try.

"There's a knack to this," he confided in her and they walked out to the parking lot. "I have my car here. I drive back home a few nights every week and always on weekends."

He wasn't as tall as Stan, and was close to her own height. Walking beside him, she gave him a friendly glance. "You're the librarian at Harvard?"

"Right," Alex agreed. "I'm the only one in the family not bowing to the pedestal of wealth. I'm not interested in making big money. I prefer being around books."

"Nothing wrong in that."

"I wish my family would agree," he said as they came up to a small, maroon foreign car. He stowed her bags in the back of it and she joined him in the narrow front seat. Soon they were heading away from the airport and taking the heavily traveled road to Marblehead.

"This is very good of you," she told him.

He was rather grim in manner, the horn-rimmed glasses giving him a solemn look. Keeping his eyes on the road, he said, "I was driving home tonight in any case. It only meant stopping by the airport."

She was thinking he had little of Stan's charm as she said, "I hope that wasn't too much of a nuisance."

"None. I wanted to get a look at you anyway. I've heard the family raving about you in the two years since they returned from Africa. I was anxious to find out if you were all that wonderful."

Beth felt her cheeks burn. "I'm sure they were merely being kind."

"No. I don't agree," he said. "I think you're an unusual type. I can see why they were impressed."

"I was impressed by them," she said. "Such a wonderful family. I felt a little jealous of their happiness."

For the first time he briefly glanced from his driving with a bitter smile for her. "You must be joking!"

"No," she said. "I'm not! I felt they got along very well."

"That isn't so true now," he said.

"Oh?" she was surprised. "I hope you're joking."

"I'm not joking," he assured her. "I've always been the despair of Mother and Father. My not wanting to make something of myself, as they say. And my disgust with money. But now both Helen and Stan have joined me in the doghouse."

"I'm startled to hear that," she said.

"Helen has gotten herself engaged to a young man socially

17

acceptable to Mother in all but one thing — he happens to be a crazy alcoholic."

"Maybe he'll reform when he marries," she suggested.

"He didn't when he was married before," the young man with the horn-rimmed glasses replied.

"That's too bad," she said. "But it may turn out differently this time."

"I doubt it," Alex said, still busy at the wheel. "And so do Mother and Dad. They don't say much, hoping Helen will change her mind on her own, but I can tell they're worried."

"Naturally they're concerned about her," she said. "That's what parents are for."

"Really?" He gave her a short mocking glance. "And then there is my brother Stan, whom you've also met."

"Yes, we've met," she agreed quietly.

"Stan has gone and gotten himself a wife the family doesn't approve of," Alex said. "And to make it worse, he's living in a nice colonial house within seeing distance of our place."

"Why should that make things worse?"

Alex smiled grimly. "You don't know the facts. Jean, that's Stan's wife, was a photographer's model in Boston. Stan met her there at a party, and you know how he is with a pretty girl."

"I'll have to take your word for it."

"He decided he'd fallen in love without finding anything out about Jean's family or her own manner of living. And let me tell you, he was in for some surprises. Her family proved to be a very ordinary lot from the Midwest, and she'd led a wild life in Boston. Marrying Stan hasn't cramped her style in the least. She's now carrying on an affair with a bachelor friend of the family who has a house next to the one lived in by Stan and her."

She was shocked. "Are you sure?"

"It's neighborhood gossip and knowledge!"

"Surely Stan could stop her somehow?"

"I suppose so. If he wanted to murder her," Alex said in a matter-of-fact way.

She gasped. "You know I didn't mean anything like that!"

"It's about all that would work," Alex said, still with his eyes on the busy road. It was dark now and the headlights of the oncoming cars were sometimes bothersome.

"He could ask her to leave and divorce her," she said.

"I doubt if she'd go. She prefers being one of the millionaire Moores and having her fun at the same time."

"Then he could move out and start divorce proceedings."

Alex nodded. "Sure. But he doesn't want to admit failure at this point. Stan is very proud, and I think he thought a lot of Jean."

"But if it is as bad as you say, he can't let it go on forever," she worried.

Alex showed a grim smile on his lean face, with the soft glow of the dashlight adding a macabre touch to his expression. "Maybe Harvey Richard will tire of her and go away. He often takes long trips. He's the neighbor to whom she's donating her charms at the moment."

"How can you joke about it?"

"I didn't mean to sound amused," he apologized. "And I can promise you it's not a joking matter for any of us. Helen is embarrassed and Mother and Father spend half their time blaming each other for not taking more interest in investigating the girl before Stan married her."

"It's too bad."

"You can believe it," Alex agreed. "So now our cozy little family group has turned out not to be so happy after all. Disillusioned?"

"I'm terribly unhappy about it," she told him. "I feel I'm coming as an intruder when you're all occupied with these problems!"

"Don't worry about it," he said. "And as far as I'm concerned, I'm rather enjoying it. I never was a member in good standing with the family. Now they can't show the same disgust for my way of life which they used to."

"That must be comforting to you," she said wryly.

"It is in a way," he replied. "And incidentally, don't let on to the others I filled you in on the family picture as it is at this moment. They mightn't appreciate it."

"I see," she said, tautly. "I'll let them reveal their troubles themselves if they decide to do it."

"Otherwise you don't know a thing," he warned her.

"I'll try to remember that," she said. "But I'll likely behave guiltily when I'm greeted by them."

"Better not," he said. "We'll soon be there."

So her first glimpse of the big stone house on the cliff had come after dark. But it was well enough spotlighted so that she could make all its details out. And the sight of it standing sternly overlooking the sea had sent a sudden chill through her. And for no reason! She should have been anticipating entering the mansion and meeting these friends she had made. But all her instincts warned her to be afraid of the house and its people. She blamed the young man at the wheel for her strange misgivings and put them down to the grim gossip he'd so blithely recounted on the drive from the airport.

He brought the car to a halt by the front door and got out and opened the car door for her. "You go in this way," he said. "I'll take your bags around to the rear and one of the servants will take them to your room."

She was trembling a little and she gave a small, panicky

laugh. "I'm being terribly childish," she said. "I think you should make the grand entrance with me."

He gave her one of his mocking looks. "Of course. I'll see you to the door," he said. "Then I'll come back to the car and take care of your luggage. Come along."

As she mounted the steps with him, she thought what a strange young man he was. And she had the feeling that for some reason he hated his family and was enjoying their present problems. She was also quite certain he'd enjoy it if anything happened to make her visit a failure. Since his parents and the others had anticipated her coming, anything which spoiled the occasion might be considered another victory by him.

She said, "At least we've gotten to know each other."

He touched his finger to the button of the electric bell and chuckled slightly. "I wouldn't count on that," was his warning.

The door was opened by the tall, prim Stephen Moore, and at once Beth was startled to see how much he'd aged in just two years. His aristocratic face had an assortment of deep new lines and wrinkles. But his pale blue eyes lit up as he took her by the hands and planted a kiss on her cheek.

"We're so pleased to have you here" he exclaimed. And then he called over his shoulder, "Andrea!"

A moment later his wife joined them in the reception foyer. She looked as distinguished as ever in the long purple gown she was wearing, but she had also aged and her delicate face seemed to have more shadowed hollows than before. It was the picture of a face racked by worry.

"Beth! How good of you to come!" the older woman said as she took her in her arms for a moment.

"Alex made everything very easy for me," she told the two. "He was waiting by the plane for me when I got off. I enjoyed getting to know him on the drive here."

Stephen Moore had closed the front door when Alex exited. Now his father looked grim. "I'm glad you found the experience pleasant," he said.

Andrea Moore hazarded a wounded smile and fluttered a thin hand nervously. "My son Alex has radical opinions which Stephen doesn't always agree with."

"I seldom approve of any opinions Alex has," the millionaire said. "Though he at least does voice a few."

"How is your father?" Andrea Moore wanted to know.

"Very well," she said. "I'm the one who was ill."

"But you have fully recovered." Stephen Moore said this as if it were a fact.

"Not fully," she told him, and saw worry cross his face.

"Yet you are able to travel?" the white-haired man queried her.

"I'm doing so on doctor's orders," she assured him. "He felt I should stay away from Africa for a few weeks or months."

"Indeed," the millionaire said looking relieved. "Then it is not catching!"

"Not at all," she said, thinking that some great change had come over these people.

It was at that moment Helen came racing down the broad central stairway to throw her arms around her and loudly proclaim her true pleasure at seeing her. It was comforting and Beth believed the brunette meant what she was saying.

For a few minutes it was all pleasant confusion. Then Helen saw her up to her room, located on the third floor with a splendid view of the ocean.

Beth took in all the charmingly furnished bedroom had to offer. She turned to the brunette girl and said, "It has a true New England flavor! Such a change for me!"

22

"I'm glad you admire it," Helen said with a crooked smile. "We call it dim Victorian grandeur, though the house is only a half-century old. It's sort of overwhelming."

"It has dignity," Beth told her, and glancing at the bed, saw her bags there. "Alex has seen to my bags so promptly."

Helen nodded, her eyes fixed on her. "I wasn't sure it was a good idea to let Alex meet you."

"Why not?"

Her friend hesitated. "He's very outspoken and radical in his views."

"I didn't mind him," she said.

"He probably was on his good behavior," was Helen's comment. "He's caused our parents lots of trouble. He was suspended from his job at the college for awhile. But Father managed to get him taken back again."

Beth said, "I find it hard to believe. When you were in Africa you became sort of a symbol to me. The happy family. I told Alex that and he seemed amused by the idea."

"He would be," Helen said. "And I'm afraid that isn't the way things really are. You were studying us with starry eyes."

"I didn't think so," she said. "I'm not all that easily impressed."

Helen smiled at her. "Thanks for having such nice opinions of us. We'll surely try to live up to them. Now I'll give you a chance to unpack and then you can join us for dinner. And by way of a special surprise, I understand Stan is going to join us."

"I'll be glad to meet Stan again and his new wife," she said politely.

Helen seemed upset. "I'm not sure that Jean will be here. In fact, I'm almost positive she won't be. She has company at the moment. A cousin from her home in the Midwest. A girl about her own age, I met her once at the shopping market just

23

this week. I think her name is Rosalie."

"Oh?" Beth said, trying to take this rush of information in a casual way. It was evident that the subject embarrassed Helen from the way she'd rambled on.

"So it will be strictly a family dinner, to honor you," Helen said.

Beth glanced at the ample diamond ring on the brunette girl's finger. "And when do I meet your fiancé?"

"Ted?" Helen said. And again she appeared uneasy. "He doesn't come here often. But you'll be bound to meet him before you leave."

"I surely hope so," she said with a smile.

Helen touched her on the arm. "But then you won't be leaving for ages. We need you here. It will be good to have someone else with us in this big house. It can be a terribly lonely place with just the family."

Beth was becoming more and more upset by what she heard. It was so evident that her conception of the Moores as a contented closely knit family couldn't have been more wrong. How could she have been so in error? What shadow had come over the family to so change things? Or had she merely been naïve? Had the family always been like this, only she was so blinded by her own desolation she hadn't been able to see it? She sighed as this seemed so obviously the answer.

Helen left her alone and she then unpacked, washed and changed into a long print skirt and silk blouse as quickly as she could. As she stood before the dresser mirror she stared at herself in it and saw that she looked wan and tense. And she knew that she was still not over the effects of her illness. It showed plainly in her face and in her emaciated body. She hoped Stan and the others would not look too closely at her, not be too critical. Especially not Stan!

24

What right had she to be so concerned about whether another woman's husband found her pleasing? She had to stop thinking of Stan in this way. It wasn't fair to either of them. The fact that his marriage was unhappy was supposed to be a secret as far as she was concerned. She wasn't supposed to know anything about it. And she must present that sort of calm front. Again she stared into the mirror and at the shadowed room behind her and wondered why this house in which she'd expected to be so content should suddenly be frightening to her? Why did she have this premonition of something dreadful happening?

She made herself believe it was merely nerves and the remnant of her illness and went down the several flights of stairs to join the family. They were gathered in the big living room waiting for her. A great log fire blazed in the fireplace at the far end of the room, and they were gathered at a bar at which Alex was presiding. But she had eyes for none of the others, for Stan was standing there in a dark suit looking as youthfully handsome as when she'd last seen him in Africa.

He came to her and took her hand. "Beth you don't know how good it is to see you."

"I've been looking forward to this moment," she heard herself say in a small voice.

He brought her a drink and then began to nervously ply her with questions about herself and her father. She replied as best she could, wondering if the others were finding it odd that they had set themselves apart this way. There was a nervous tension underlining the conversation and giving it a quite different tone from the very ordinary words they were exchanging. It was as if they were satisfying a hunger which overpowered them, and when they had to follow the others in to the dining room it was with regret.

She sat at the table with Alex at her side and Stan across

from her. She was sure the dour Alex was studying her with grim humor from behind those horn-rimmed glasses, and she was so uneasy that she was aware of only a minor part of the dinner small talk. Her brief moments with Stan had convinced her of one thing, that he was desperately unhappy and in need of sympathy, which he was apparently not getting from his family.

Once Stephen Moore addressed himself to her and told her, "In a few days Andrea and I shall be celebrating our thirtieth wedding anniversary. Would you believe that possible? If it weren't for all these grown-up youngsters of ours, I'd say it was only a couple of years ago that we were married!"

"That's charming of you and sentimental, Stephen," his frail wife had replied form her end of the table. "But I'm afraid I feel the weight of the years more than you do."

"Nonsense!" her husband protested.

Beth made a suitably polite congratulation to them and the talk went on. When dinner was over, Stan caused her more uneasiness by taking her aside again.

He must have seen she was embarrassed for he said, "Don't worry, I'm leaving. I have to go early. But I do want to see you again. I want to see you alone. Somewhere away from the family!"

She gave him a troubled look. "You're married, Stan. I don't think we ought to plan an assignation."

"Don't be so stupidly proper," Stan said almost angrily. "We happen to be two adults who are friends. There is no reason why we shouldn't meet and have a quiet talk."

"Perhaps," she wavered. "I've only just arrived."

"And I've been counting the days until you got here," Stan said in his serious manner. "I'll phone you and tell you when I can come by and pick you up."

"We'll see," she said.

They were standing near the foot of the broad winding stairway by a table heaped with fine antique silver and other items. At that moment Alex came by and as if to divert any suspicions his brother might have, Stan hastily picked up a heavy silver candlestick and held the ornate piece before her with a smile.

"Part of the family heritage," he said, obviously for the benefit of passing Alex. "Look at the exquisite pattern and consider its weight!"

She knew that he was play-acting, that this was a charade for his brother's benefit. But she forgot this as a different, terrifying feeling came over her. Staring at the dark young man standing there holding the candlestick in his hand like a weapon, a surge of fear shot through her! The expression on Stan's face seemed to have subtly changed so that his smile had taken on a macabre overtone, and his eyes showed a sinister light which made her gasp! He looked like a man contemplating a murder.

Chapter Two

The weird illusion lasted for only a brief moment. Then the macabre feeling left her and she was staring at a pleasant young man holding a candlestick in his hands for her to study. And it was he who was now looking at her with amazement.

"What's wrong?" he wanted to know.

"Nothing," she said weakly. How could she reveal the sinister thoughts which had come to her a moment before?

"You're very pale!" Stan said. "And a few seconds ago you were staring at me with a kind of horrified look. I don't know what Alex will think I said to you." He referred to his brother, who had gone on up the stairway.

She touched a hand to her temple. In a small voice, she said, "For a moment I didn't feel well."

"Are you all right now?"

"Yes. It passed quickly."

Stan frowned. "We have a good doctor if you need one."

She shook her head. "No. It's just the old illness. I've been warned that it will take time to fully recover. I have had a long tiring day."

"And I've not helped," Stan said contritely. "I'm sorry." He put the candlestick back on the table. "I'll be on my way now and you'll hear from me later."

"All right."

He hesitated. "If you don't feel better get Mother to call our doctor. He's excellent or I wouldn't suggest it."

"I will," she promised.

28

"Goodnight, then," he said and turned from her awkwardly. She watched as he said goodnight to his parents and then left.

Helen came to her with a knowing smile. "I saw you and Stan were making up for the two years you've been apart," his sister said.

Beth said, "I enjoyed seeing him again."

"And he enjoyed seeing you."

"I'm glad he was able to come," she said lamely.

Helen sighed. "So am I. I think he has reached a point of desperation with his wife. I don't know what will happen or how he and Jean will work out their problems."

She said, "Surely if they love each other . . ."

"I doubt if Jean ever cared for him," Helen interrupted. "How could she behave as she has if there were any love or respect on her part?"

"It's that bad?"

"That bad."

"I'm sorry," she said.

"I shouldn't have mentioned it," Helen apologized. "But I could tell he was so happy with you. He's rarely like that these days. If Jean keeps on, I'm terrified of his doing something violent."

Though Helen could not possibly know it, these words had a frightening implication for Beth. The moment of sheer horror when she'd briefly seen Stan as a murderer came back with ominous swiftness. And at once she worried that she might in some eerie way have foreseen the future.

Finding her voice, she said, "Stan would never harm anyone."

"I wouldn't expect so," Helen said soberly. "But then one wonders just how much a person can stand."

The conversation was interrupted by Helen's father and

mother joining them. They went into the living room and sat and talked about remembered things in Botswana until the time came to retire. Then Beth said her goodnights to them all and went up to her third-floor room. It was a calm, moonlight night and she stood by the window gazing out at the ocean for some time, trying to set her thoughts in order.

In the semi-darkness and silence of her room much of the fear she'd known earlier in the night came back to her. In the distance the ocean waves washed against the rocks and sand with a roar that faded only to return again. Her terror came and went in almost the same manner. At last she forced herself to leave the window and begin to prepare for bed.

But even in bed she was not able to relax. Sleep eluded her as she thought of Stan and his problem with his wayward wife. Why hadn't he waited for her? Or come back to Africa to talk it out with her? There had never even been a letter from him and he had married this other girl — a girl who did not love him and who was driving him to the point of desperation!

Now he wanted to turn to her for help and sympathy, but had she any right to listen to him? Not really. And yet she knew that she probably would. And she dared not think what might come of it. She debated packing quickly the next morning and going back to Bermuda after making some excuse to the Moores. At least then she would be safe.

How ironical it was that she should have sought out this family as a refuge from her own illness and problems only to discover that they were worse off than herself. Wearily she closed her eyes and then sleep came at last. But with it the nightmare which had tortured her for so long.

Once again her mother was leaving her. She began the terrified search for her in the forest, frightened and bewildered. Again she was threatened by dark terror which made her twist in agony beneath the sheets and again there was the haunting feeling of loss as she plaintively cried out her mother's name to get no reply. But this time her nightmare took a different turn! Rather than hearing her father's voice in the background, she saw Stan in the dream. A distance from her in the jungle he stood watching her with sad eyes. But she was not able to find her way to him or he to join her. Whenever she tried to reach him, she lost her way. And so the nightmare ended as usual. She wakened with a scream and then lay there weak and perspiring.

She worried that her scream might have disturbed the others in the mansion. But all was silence and she decided that the walls were thick enough to have muffled the sound of her voice. For this she was grateful. But she knew that her stay with the Moores was not going to be the pleasant experience she had so long anticipated. She tried to find comfort by telling herself that in life this was often the case. But it was cold comfort.

The next morning she awoke to find that fog had settled in along the coast to make a grim, gray day. In a way it was a day to match her own mood. But she determined to keep a cheerful front for the Moores no matter what she felt. She owed that much to them for their kindness in taking her into their home.

At breakfast she and Helen shared the table. Helen explained, "My father always has his breakfast in his office in Boston. Mother takes hers in her room upstairs and Alex only has coffee before he leaves."

Beth smiled at her. "So we are the only two regular breakfast eaters?"

"That's about. it. I've had my breakfast alone almost every morning until now. I'm glad to have company."

Beth paused over her orange juice. "The fog surprised me. I had no idea it could come in this thick or so quickly."

"We get heavy fogs here," Helen said. "I hope it doesn't depress you. It's a change from the African sun."

"It's probably just what I need," she told the other girl. "After long days of endless hot sun, fog can be welcome."

Helen eyed her solicitously. "How do you feel? Last night I thought you were very pale and weary."

"I was," she answered quietly.

"You look much better this morning. More rested."

"I had a tiring day yesterday," she said.

"Of course you did," Helen agreed. "As soon as the weather is better here I'll show you around the town. It is ancient and very quaint in sections and we have a lot of fine homes."

"I'm sure you do," Beth said. "You say Stan's place is along the cliffs as well?"

Helen nodded. "Less than a half-mile from here. You can see it on a clear day. A pleasant white colonial."

Beth paused in buttering some toast to ask, "Has your family always lived here?"

The other girl smiled. "Mother has. My father came to this area after they were married. They had a modest home at first and then they bought this place after father became really wealthy."

"It's a majestic house," Beth said.

"More like a big museum than a home," Beth said with a hint of distaste in her tone. "I've often suggested to Father that he donate it to the town and find us something more cozy."

"He's probably devoted to it."

"He is," Helen agreed, "so I doubt he will let it go in his lifetime. It is perhaps a sort of status symbol with him. You

32

see he isn't the blueblood of the family. Mother is."

"Oh?"

"Yes," Helen went on as though it was a favorite subject with her. "Mother is a Kimball. One of the oldest families in this part of the world. The Kimballs are all socially prominent and most of them wealthy. Father, on the other hand, is strictly one of the new rich as far as they're concerned."

"I'm sure it is all very unimportant to either your father or mother," Beth said.

Helen looked thoughtful. "I can't really say. Perhaps Mother still feels strongly about traditional things to a greater extent than the rest of us. Alex leading his hippie existence and getting into trouble several times has upset her more than it has Father."

"He is a different sort from Stan," Beth agreed.

"Entirely different. He won't have anything to do with Father's business activities and I don't really think he pays proper attention to his university job."

Beth was thinking about the cynical comments the young man had made to her on the drive to Marblehead. In that short time he had filled her in on many facts about the family and shattered a lot of the views she'd held about them. But she daren't let Helen know how indiscreet her brother's conversation had been.

The fog continued to cloak the district and after breakfast Beth moved from room to room downstairs viewing the fine furnishings of the mansion. The collection of paintings on the walls and the many rare prints were an attraction in themselves. She was in the study giving particular attention to a series of framed Hogarths when she heard someone come into the room behind her.

She turned and saw that it was Andrea Moore. She smiled at the older woman and said, "I've been admiring your art collection. These Hogarths must be very old and valuable."

"They are," Andrea Moore said with some pride. "I received them as a bequest from my grandmother and I was happy to get them."

"I can believe that," she agreed. "You have so many fine things in this house."

The frail woman's worn face showed a look of timid pleasure. "The Boston *Globe* came here a few years ago and took photos and wrote an interesting article on the place."

"How wonderful."

"It was when our children were younger," Andrea said with a sigh. "I think we were all much happier then. I don't think Stephen or the others appreciate the treasures surrounding us here. But I do. I look on these things as a symbol of a gracious way of life. A way of life that seems to be fast disappearing."

Beth said, "Not while there are still people like you left."

"I often feel there are not so many who care," Andrea Moore said with a sigh.

"I had no idea the place would be so large," Beth said.

"It's probably too large," the older woman said. "But my husband likes it, so I imagine we will continue to live on here until Helen and Alex marry and leave us."

Beth nodded. "That will change things. I suppose Stan being married has made a difference."

A strange expression came into the older woman's pale blue eyes and her thin face clouded. "It has made a profound difference," she said in a quiet tone.

Beth could not miss the change that had so suddenly showed in the older woman. And she remembered what Helen had said earlier about her mother feeling more strongly about any disgrace to the family than anyone else. It was all too likely that Andrea Moore was suffering almost as much as

Stan from his wife's disgraceful affair with a family friend.

Wanting to change the subject Beth said quickly, "I believe you'll be celebrating your thirtieth anniversary soon."

Stan's mother smiled. "Yes. Some friends are having a party to celebrate our wedding anniversary next week."

"Mr. Moore mentioned it. He seemed very pleased."

"We are," Andrea agreed. "We're looking forward to the affair. And do make yourself at home here. We so much want you to enjoy your visit."

"You've been far too kind to me," Beth said, meaning it.

The rest of the day and night passed uneventfully, except that Beth continued to be plagued by her recurring nightmare. But she was gradually becoming more rested and feeling like herself. The next day the sun returned and it was one of those perfect warm fall days which all too often precede a storm.

"Today we must make a tour of the town," Helen told her.

And they did. Beth enjoyed the quaint New England town with its mixture of new and old. And at the end of the tour they drove back along the cliffs and Helen pointed out Stan's house in passing.

Slowing the car, she indicated a huge white colonial on their left, saying, "That is Stan's place."

Beth stared at it. "It is large though nothing like your own mansion."

Helen laughed ruefully. "It doesn't do to compare our place with any of the others in town. But you're right. Stan bought himself a good-sized house."

"I don't see any sign of anyone near it," she said as they drove on.

"You never see Jean out around," Helen said in a dry

voice. "She's a night creature."

Beth thought it unwise to pry any further and let the subject drop. But she remembered Stan's promise to call her and it made her rather edgy since she didn't know what she should do about it.

As it turned out, she didn't have too much time to debate the question in her mind. The phone call came late that afternoon and one of the maids summoned her to the phone.

Guessing who it was before she picked up the phone, she began with a nervous, "Yes?"

"It's Stan," came the familiar voice from the other end of the line. "I want to see you tonight."

"I don't know," she hesitated.

"I won't accept a refusal," he told her. "I'll come by the house around eight. It will be dark by then. I won't come in. It would be easier all around if you came out on the steps and waited for me."

"What will I tell the others?"

"You don't have to say anything," Stan told her. "Just slip away from them and come down one of the side stairways. They'll think you're in your room resting or that you've gone for a stroll."

"I'll feel guilty."

"No need."

"Can't I even tell Helen?"

"No. I'd rather you didn't," Stan said. "Don't forget. Eight o'clock."

"I'll think about it," she said nervously.

There was a short moment of silence at the other end of the line and then he warned her, "If you're not there, I'll come in and get you. I don't mind the others knowing. I'm only carrying on this secrecy because you seem to want it."

"Please," she protested. "I'll do my best to be there."

"That's better," Stan said. And he hung up.

The whole business had an abruptness which left her a little stunned. She was about to put down the phone when she heard the click of an extension from some other area of the house being put back in place and knew that their conversation had been overheard by someone. Someone had been interested in what they were saying. But who?

This bothered her for the rest of the day. But she felt she would have to see Stan alone just once and try and settle some of the things between them. At least she had to give him a chance to say whatever he wanted to.

That evening neither Alex nor his father returned from Boston. Alex was staying in his rooms in town for the night and Stephen Moore had some sort of business function that would mean a late return to Marblehead. So Beth had dinner with only Helen and her mother at the table. This made things easier.

After dinner Andrea Moore went directly upstairs to her room and Helen went out to keep a date with her fiancé, Ted. Beth had hoped that Ted might come by the house and so give her a chance to meet him. But it seemed the two were meeting at one of the yacht clubs.

As eight o'clock drew near she found herself becoming tense. She worried that Stan's mother might come back downstairs and make it awkward for her to get away. But this didn't happen. So as the time to meet Stan arrived she hurried upstairs and put on a coat and tied a kerchief over her head. She was especially sensitive to the cold after her long stay in Africa.

She came back down and went directly out to the verandah where she waited for the lights of Stan's car to appear in the broad paved driveway. When she saw them she hurried down the steps and over to the car. He had the door open for her and she hastily got in beside him.

He drove away at once with a grim smile for her as he gazed at her for a brief moment. "I thought you'd show up," he said.

She stared at his rather handsome profile as the soft light of the dash reflected on him and saw nothing of the evil that had so frightened her for a moment a few nights back. He didn't look like a possible murderer now but rather like a perfectly ordinary, serious young man — the young man she'd come to know and like back in Botswana.

With a sigh, she said, "I'm not sure I should be here."

"I'd expect that kind of viewpoint from my mother," he told her crisply. "You're supposed to be a modern young woman."

"I am," she said. "But I don't think I should mix myself up in your problems."

He was watching the road ahead as he drove. "Does that mean you no longer have any interest in me?"

"No."

"Well, then?"

"I mean you have a wife. And whatever trouble there may be between you, I shouldn't interfere."

"I'm not asking you to interfere," Stan said grimly. "I just need to talk to someone. And you are the one."

"I see," she said.

"Don't sound so gloomy," he told her. "I know a nice little eating place on the road to Boston where we can sit in a dark corner and talk to our heart's delight without causing any scandal."

"I hope you're right," she said, not yet sold on the idea.

He pulled the car off the roadway before a long, one-story restaurant and lounge with a large neon sign labeling it THE WUNDER BAR. As he turned off the motor he smiled at her and said, "It's not any grand place, but it will do for our purpose."

She went into the restaurant with him and was glad to note that it was almost empty. They were shown to a stall in the dark corner which Stan had promised to find for them. He ordered drinks and then began a serious conversation.

Studying her solemnly across the table, he said, "First, let me make it clear this isn't just a case of someone wanting a disinterested party to tell their troubles to."

"No?"

"No. I wouldn't demean you or myself by doing that. I'm here to tell you about Jean and me because I've realized too late that I'm in love with you."

"Stan!" she protested.

"Wait," he said, "let me finish. I made a mess of things by taking you at your word. You said you wouldn't leave your father for a husband and I believed you. I shouldn't have. I ought to have gone back to Botswana and stayed there until you agreed to marry me."

She smiled faintly. "That could have taken quite a while."

"I oughtn't to have worried about it," Stan said. "Instead I tried to forget you. And part of forgetting you was my involving myself with Jean. She was and is a beauty and for a while we had fun. All the time she was out to marry me and exploit me!"

"What makes you so sure of that?"

Stan's face was grim with suppressed anger. "I've found out all about her. About her present and her past. She wasn't married to me six months when she began this affair with Harvey Richard. A man I've known all my life. His family and my mother's are even intermarried. You can imagine the gossip that is going on in the town "

"Can't you stop her?"

"She denies everything and still carries on behind my back. I've even tried to discuss it with Harvey, but he naturally backs up her denials. There is no way! I married a corrupt woman. If it weren't Harvey it would be someone else!"

"There must be something you can do!"

Stan gave her a significant look. "I could murder her!"

And for just a fleeting moment she saw that frightening look of a killer on his handsome face again and felt another surge of fear.

"You mustn't say such things or even think them!" she told him in a hushed voice.

"It could be the one way out."

"You're mad! Divorce her! Have her divorce you! Make some kind of settlement! Pay her what she wants! It would be worth anything to be rid of her if she's the sort of woman you describe."

Stan looked forlorn. "She doesn't want a divorce. She likes the cloak of respectability the Moore name gives her. She's willing to go on a lifetime like this. Even though I know about her and what she's doing. She doesn't care for me as a person so it makes no difference."

"Surely enough money would make her change her mind!"

"I doubt it," Stan said grimly. "And then I haven't all that much cash of my own without turning to Father or Mother. And you know how they feel about my marriage. They would never give Jean their money!"

She saw the despair in him and worried even more. "You'll have to be patient," she told him. "Learn how to wait. Your wife will tire of all this sooner or later and then she'll be willing to talk terms with you."

He gave her a tragic look. "Now that you are here, I have

no more patience. I want you! I want us to have a life together."

"I have to return to Africa soon," she said. "Even if we had plans I'd have to go back to Dad for awhile. So there is lots of time for us. I'm not going to make any rash decisions. And you can try to find a way to cope with your problem."

"My problem is simple," he said in a heavy tone. "Just get rid of Jean."

She looked at him urgently. "You mustn't think of violence."

"I can't help it, living under the same roof with her, her presence a constant torment."

"Ignore it or move out," she said.

Stan went on unhappily, "And now she has a cousin of hers with us. The same type as herself. They even talk the same way and think alike. If Jean gave her a chance I wouldn't doubt this Rosalie would make a play for Harvey herself. She's that kind of person!"

"You don't have to have her in your house, do you?"

"I've had a row with Jean about her today. I said she'd have to go. And for once Jean agreed with me. I think she has a clue that Rosalie is out to take Harvey from her. She said she'd ask her to leave."

"So that will be settled."

"If Jean lives up to her word. She's not all that good at it!"

Beth reached out and touched his hand. "You're allowing yourself to panic. This isn't like you. If you face up to this problem as you would to a business problem, you'd handle it a lot better."

He shook his head. "Too many emotions involved. I guess Alex has the best of it. He's walked out on the family to a good extent and he's not interested in the family money. He may be a rebel but at least he's doing his own thing."

"It doesn't seem to have done much for him but make him bitter," she pointed out.

Stan said, "We're all making messes of our lives. Helen is sure to marry Ted. She thinks she can reform him. I could tell her now he's not that kind of an alcoholic!"

"Why has it turned out this way?" she wondered. "I thought you such a solid family group."

"We're anything but that," he said. "We're all at odds."

"I shouldn't stay away too long," she told him.

"When can we meet again?" he wanted to know.

"We can't," she said. "Not until you solve your problems with Jean."

"That's not fair!"

"It is," she insisted. "You've told me everything. There's no easy answer. You've got to take time and work it out gradually."

Stan looked tense. "Patience isn't my forte."

She felt the tautness in him and said, "It had better be."

"I make no promises."

"I'll see you at the house," she said, trying to put him off easily. "You'll be visiting and we can talk there."

His eyes were tragic. "It's a torment for me to be with you and have to play act casualness for the others."

"We can manage," she said. "Now let us go."

Stan paid the check and they left. In the car he took her in his arms and gently kissed her and held her for a long while. She let him do this because it seemed right and she hoped that it might give him proof of her sincerity. Perhaps now he might be willing to wait and plan a means for his freedom — a means short of the murder he so casually threatened.

While he drove her back to his father's mansion he was oddly silent and this worried her. And so did his manner when they parted. He seemed all at once to have shrunk within himself. He no longer seemed to want to reveal his inner torment to her. There was no kiss between them as he saw her to the door; just a muted goodnight.

She waited in the cold of the verandah to see him get into the car and drive away. Then filled with misgivings about what might be on the tormented young man's mind, she opened the door and went inside.

The reception foyer was in darkness. And as she closed the door behind her, she was all at once conscious of a spectral shadow looming up beside. She stepped back with a gasp of shock!

"Don't be afraid!" It was the voice of Stan's mother.

Relieved that the ghostly figure was merely Andrea Moore in her dressing gown, Beth said, "You appeared so suddenly you gave me a start!"

"I didn't mean to," the older woman said. "I was watching from the living room window and I saw you and my son."

She stood there embarrassed. "We went out to a roadside place to talk."

"I understand," Stan's mother said. "My poor Stan!"

"He is in a very desperate frame of mind," she agreed. "I saw him because I hoped I might be able to help."

"That dreadful Jean!" Andrea Moore said tensely. "I've talked to my husband and asked him to try and do something. But he refuses to interfere. He says it is Stan's problem."

"I suppose that is true," Beth said. "Still he does need to know that others care."

"It was kind of you to see him and talk with him," the older woman said gently. "I hope you were able to help him."

"I told him to be patient," she said. "That time might help bring about a solution."

"That was good advice," Stan's mother agreed. She hesitated before she added, "If only he had married you."

"That isn't the problem now."

"If he had married you there would have been no problem," the older woman said. "Both his father and I liked you so much, we'd hoped something would come of your meeting."

Beth sighed. "I was probably partly to blame for that failure," she admitted. "But I've told Stan I do care for him and I'm willing to wait and see what happens."

"How kind you are," Andrea said with what seemed deep sincerity. And she placed a frail arm around Beth and kissed her on the cheek. "I'm sure that one day you and my son will have a life together."

It was a touching scene and one which helped Beth lose a good part of her guilt feelings. She said goodnight to the troubled mother and went on up to her own room. That night she slept without any of the strange dreams which had troubled her for so long.

But things did not work out as she'd hoped. In the days that followed Stan made no appearance at his father's house. So she had no chance to speak with him. This bothered her a good deal and once she heard his mother phoning him and talking to him a long while. Beth hoped that she might at least get a phone call from him but she didn't.

Helen tried to pass it off lightly. "Stan must be terribly busy," she said. "I can't imagine his not calling on us otherwise."

"He probably is," she'd agreed politely, though she guessed being busy had nothing to do with his continued absence.

Stephen Moore made no comment about Stan's keeping out of the way, but Alex was not so kind when he returned home for the weekend. He waited until he met Beth out walking along the cliffs. There above the roar of the ocean and the frothing of the waves on the beach he confronted her with a crooked smile.

"Out for your health?" he'd asked.

She faced him with a mild defiance. "I felt a walk would do me good."

"I'm always anxious to get out of that place," he said, indicating the mansion in the background with a nod.

"But you keep coming back to it," she reminded him.

"A bad habit. I won't one day," he said. "I'm caught now. The folks expect me to stay on for their anniversary party tomorrow night."

"I'd almost forgotten about it."

"I wish I could."

"I suppose you'll all be there," she said, thinking that she might see Stan when he came to join the others. It might provide a brief meeting for them at least.

The cold eyes behind the horn-rimmed glasses showed a malicious glint. Alex said, "I understand Stan isn't joining the happy party. There could be questions asked as to why his wife wasn't there as well. So he prefers not to attend."

"That's too bad," she said, glancing out at the ocean to avoid his continued stare.

In a taunting voice, Alex added, "I guess you're disappointed. You've been counting on seeing him."

She turned on him angrily. "What do you mean?"

"Don't pretend," the thin young man told her. "We all know he's been keeping away from the house lately. That has to be because of you. What happened? Did you two have a quarrel?"

"That's none of your business!" she retorted.

He chuckled unpleasantly. "I guess that's what happened!"

"You know nothing about it!"

"A poor time for you to put Stan down," his brother said in a gloating voice. "He's in a bad state of mind. Having trouble with you could push him over the brink!"

"No!" her protest was one of anguish. The sly Alex had hit a nerve!

"You must realize that," Alex persisted. "He's about ready to throttle Jean. He's even talked about it."

"How can you hate everyone so?" Beth demanded tearfully. Unable to bear her tormenter any longer, she turned and ran back across the lawn toward the imposing mansion which housed so much strife.

The next mention of the anniversary party came from Helen. She approached her about it the following morning at the breakfast table. "We're all attending the party for Father and Mother at the yacht club tonight," she said. "And you're invited as well."

She shook her head. "Thanks. No. I don't feel up to it. I had a bad night last night and my head is reeling today."

Helen looked worried. "Is there anything I can do?"

"No. It's the old trouble. I've been warned I will have minor bouts of the fever for months. It will go gradually."

"Can I call our doctor?"

"It's not that bad," she said, reassuringly. "But I'm certain I'd be much wiser to remain here quietly reading or watching television for the evening."

Helen looked disappointed. "We'd all like you to attend. If you feel better, be sure and come with us."

"I will," Beth promised.

But she knew there was no chance of it. Not only did she think she would be uneasy at the party, but she was truly not feeling well. She blamed it mostly on the tormenting by Alex and a night of wild dreams which had followed the confrontation with the bitter young man.

There was also a hint in her condition of a recurring fever bout. She took a double dose of her medicine as the doctor had advised in this event and hoped that within a few hours her condition would improve. But her optimism wasn't justified. Instead she gradually felt worse, so much so that she went up to her bedroom and stayed there. Rather than come down for lunch she had a tray of simple food sent up to her. And she wasn't able to touch any of that except the tea.

At the same time the weather had taken a turn for the worse. The previous day and all that morning had been dull gray and strangely mild and calm. She'd vaguely heard reports about a threatened hurricane along the Northeast coast but hadn't paid much attention to them. But at midday a heavy rain began and there was a tremendous wind with it. Darkness came early along with the lashing storm which made even the solid old mansion creak and the shutters by its windows clatter.

Stretched out on her bed reading a mystery novel, Beth didn't at once realize how truly bad the storm was. Then Helen came to her room dressed to leave. And Stan's brunette sister told her, "It's storming out terribly! We'll get drenched just getting in and out of the car! And it is predicted to end before the evening is over! Just our bad luck that it should be at its peak now!"

Beth raised herself on an elbow and said, "I'm sorry." And then added weakly, "You look lovely!"

Helen stood by the bed looking troubled. "I'm worried about you. You seem so ill. I don't like leaving you alone. And you will be alone! This is the servants' night off. Are you sure you don't want me to stay?"

"No. I wouldn't think of keeping you from the party."

"Being sure you're looked after is more important," Helen

47

said. "I'd have had the housekeeper stay if I'd known you were so ill. I'm sure she would have even if the others were taking the night off."

"Please go! Don't keep your parents waiting," she begged the other girl. "I'll manage very well."

Helen left reluctantly. Once again Beth lay back on the bed. The novel slid out of her hands as obviously she would not manage as well as she thought. This time the fever was really hitting her. Her moans mingled with the shrieking of the wind and the drive of the rain against the windows of the dark room.

She felt herself sinking into the dark depths of unconsciousness and for a while all was a black velvet silence. Then she became vaguely aware of the storm sounds once more. And suddenly above them she was sure she heard the frantic scream of a woman! Eyes wide, the perspiration trickling down her temples, she lifted herself weakly on an elbow and listened. And the shrieking came again! Closer this time! Just under her windows!

Chapter Three

Beth sat up in bed with effort. The howling of the wind and the lashing of the heavy rain had risen to new heights. Yet she was sure that above the fury of the storm she'd heard that feminine scream. Her fever-blurred mind found it difficult to cope with the situation. But she felt she should try to get downstairs and find out what was happening.

Slowly she swung her legs out from under the coverings and braced herself to stand. It was an effort in her weakened state. And when she finally did get to her feet, she swayed in an alarming manner and felt she might collapse. She stood there in the subdued light of the upper bedroom in the storm-lashed old mansion trying desperately to clear her muddled mind. But the fever had taken its toll and she felt weak and helpless.

Her slim young body trembled and great beads of perspiration poured from her. Her pretty face wore a frightened look and her glazed eyes tried to bring her surroundings into focus without success. Then she heard a second scream! This one came from somewhere below in the mansion. And it roused her into an effort to leave the room.

Groping her way as if in a thick fog, she headed for the door leading to the hallway. Grasping its handle weakly she opened it and went out into the near darkness. She had only a vague idea of the direction she was taking. She hoped that she was heading for the landing. Her step was uncertain and she was still trembling. But finally she did reach the head of the

49

broad stairs. Gripping the railing she began to descend the stairs one at a time.

After what seemed an endless time she reached the lower landing which was only three steps above the level of the living room. The living room was brightly lighted in contrast to the hall upstairs and as she stood there clinging to the railing she sought some sign of the woman who had screamed. But the room seemed to be empty.

The outside sounds of the storm became apparent to her again and she began to wonder if in her fever-stricken state her mind hadn't taken to playing tricks on her. She'd known weird fantasies during her fever bouts back in Africa. But this recurrence was something new. The elegantly furnished living room swirled before her glazed eyes and she was about to try and return upstairs again when she heard a third loud female scream!

From a doorway on the left a woman in a black gown came running. She appeared to be in a hysterical state and came straight across the room so that she was only a few yards from the landing on which Beth stood. The girl had long, blonde hair which flowed around the bare shoulders revealed by the gown's thin straps. She had a square, strong-featured face with large blue eyes, fairly wide apart. Beth thought her lovely in the glamorous mold of a model. But now the loveliness of the model's face was disfigured by fear!

Beth had barely taken in all this when a man came hurrying into the room following the girl. It was Stan Moore, and his handsome face was contorted with rage. He went directly to the beautiful blonde girl who had backed to a table by the bottom of the stairs and was cowering from him there. Angry words were exchanged between them and Stan brutally slapped the girl across the face. The blonde screamed again and began sobbing. Beth was frozen where she stood by her weakness but she also cried out to Stan to stop quarreling with the girl.

Of course he paid no attention to her. It was as if she'd not been there at all; as if this melodrama she was watching were being played out on a screen before her. She was merely a bemused spectator. The quarrel continued with the blonde lashing back at Stan and her fingernails leaving bloody lines on his cheek. Now there was a gleam of madness in the young man's eyes as he reached out and seized something from the table and held it high to strike the blonde!

Beth recognized the makeshift weapon! It was the identical candlestick which Stan had held in his hands on the day of her arrival at the mansion. She remembered the certain light he'd had in his eyes then and the eerie feeling it had given her. Now she was seeing the candlestick used for violence!

"Stop! Don't!" she cried out, knowing her voice was too weak to be heard above the sounds of the storm from outside.

Stan lurched toward the blonde as she made a futile effort to escape. He caught her by one wrist and then swung the heavy silver candlestick with his free hand. It caught her on the side of the head with a sickening blow. Her expression of fear changed to one of dull surprise as blood spurted from her temple and she collapsed to the floor. Stan stood over her grimly, the candlestick still in his hand.

"What have you done?" Beth cried out, clinging to the railing for support.

He turned to stare up at her, his dark hair awry, his handsome face distorted with rage. "It had to end this way," he said tautly.

Her eyes wandered from him to the crumpled body at his feet and then the room began to whirl wildly around her and it all became a hopeless blur. She glanced at him again and tried to speak but no words came. Next she lost consciousness.

She came to in a hospital bed. The white, antiseptic walls of the room reflected the cold, autumn sunlight. She had no idea how long she'd been there or even how she'd gotten there. And for a few minutes she had no recollection of her illness and that night of terror. Then it came rushing back to her in a flood of grim remembrance!

She'd seen Stan Moore kill a beautiful young woman! She'd been in her bedroom trying to concentrate on a mystery novel and failing because of her recurrence of fever. There had been a bad storm. And then from outside in the storm she'd heard a woman's scream. She'd somehow managed to get downstairs to find out what the scream meant and she'd been a witness to a murder!

It was a terrifying thought and she wondered what had happened after her collapse. Had Stan called the police and asked for an ambulance to take her to the hospital? Had he confessed his crime and seen that she received proper medical attention? What of the family and their reaction? Had the murder made headlines in the media?

Beth thought the svelte blonde girl she'd seen murdered must have been Stan's wife. He'd finally been taunted too much by the lovely but promiscuous Jean and had murdered her in a moment of rage. He'd threatened doing this in the past and some new act of Jean's must have spurred him to it. How would the Moore family survive the disgrace of the incident? And how would the law deal with Stan? Not too harshly, she hoped, knowing how he'd been tried.

She still felt weak but her head was clear. The recurrence of the fever must have passed. Now she was only concerned with what had happened the night of her collapse and how

Stan might fare. She wondered if she would be called on as a witness and how much about the crime was known.

In the midst of her troubled speculations the door of the hospital room opened and a middle-aged nurse in white uniform and cap entered. Seeing that Beth had regained consciousness, the nurse came over to her bedside with a smile.

"Well, this is a nice surprise," the nurse said. "You've come back to us."

"Just a few minutes ago," she said weakly. "How long have I been here?"

The nurse said, "You were brought here the night before last. You were completely out of it. Luckily the Moores knew about your fever history and were able to tell the doctor. That made it easier to treat you."

"I've had these spells before," she said. "I was warned they might continue for a year or two."

"The doctors weren't too worried," the nurse said. "As soon as they understood your illness, they knew what to expect. You must feel terribly weak."

"I do," she admitted. And then cautiously, she asked, "What about the Moores?"

"One or the other of them have been here almost constantly," the nurse said with a smile. There was no hint that she knew of the murder in her manner. This was puzzling.

Beth said, "I could hardly expect them to be so concerned."

"They are. But they're fine people. One of our best families."

Beth was becoming more and more curious. There was surely nothing in the nurse's manner to suggest that news of the murder had become public. Yet she didn't know how it could have been kept a secret. Then she began to think that perhaps the nurse was deliberately keeping any mention of the tragedy from her in order not to shock her.

Beth said, "I remember it was storming very badly the night I took ill."

The nurse nodded. "Yes. It was a hurricane. An oddity. We don't usually get them that bad at this time of year."

"Do you know who found me after I collapsed?" she asked. "All the Moore family were attending an anniversary dinner. And the servants were out. I was alone in the house." It was a carefully phrased question to try and bring out some mention of the murder.

The nurse accepted her question casually. "I believe it was Stanley Moore who found you. He hadn't attended the party and happened to call at his parents' home."

So it was Stan who had found her! Her tensions rose! But what about the rest of it? Seemingly he'd somehow managed to cover up the killing of his wife. Or perhaps the injury to the blonde Jean had not been as serious as she'd thought and the girl had recovered and the entire incident had been hushed up.

She asked, "What time is it?"

"Two o'clock," the nurse said. "I'll let the doctor know you've come to and he'll be in to see you shortly. And if any of the Moores come to visit you, I'll let them in for a few minutes, if the doctor gives permission."

"Please do," she begged in a weary voice.

"Don't overdo," the nurse warned. "Just take it easy."

Beth was still far too weak to do anything else. The doctor came and was professionally cheerful about her condition. It might be three or four days before she could leave the hospital but a week should see her fully recovered. The possibility of another recurrence would be lessened as time passed. Still there was no hint that anything was known publicly of the drama which had taken place at the old mansion

54

the night of the storm.

She tried not to torment herself with thoughts about it. One of the Moores would surely arrive soon and then she would hear all that had happened. Unless they discreetly had agreed to keep her in the dark about the affair. They might have done this if Jean had made a quick recovery. But could anyone have survived that awful blow from the heavy candlestick of gleaming silver?

Some time after the doctor visited her the door from the hallway opened and Helen Moore came in. Helen looked delighted and came over to her bedside with a smile.

Bending down to kiss her, Helen said, "It's so good to see you like yourself again. I was beginning to get very worried about you in spite of the doctors' optimism."

"I've caused you so much trouble," Beth said, gazing up at her.

"Nonsense," her friend replied. "You couldn't help getting ill. I should never have left you the other night. It was just good luck that Stan came by and found you. Then he had a terrible time getting the ambulance to come for you in the storm."

Again there was this confirmation that Stan had come to the house and found her collapsed. But no mention of his wife, Jean, or the attack he'd made on her.

Carefully, she asked, "Was Stan alone when he found me?"

Without hesitation Helen nodded. "Yes. He came by to inquire how the anniversary party had gone. But we weren't home yet. And according to him, you had come down the stairs and were standing on the lower landing. He started over to you, aware that you were ill, and you collapsed before he could reach you."

Beth listened with fear. It was all just as it had happened, except that Stan had carefully omitted any mention of Jean or of his attack on her. Apparently he'd not killed her and had somehow gotten her out of the house and back to his own place. "I owe Stan a special debt," she said. "I must thank him."

Beth looked wary. "He's away for a week or so. But I'm sure he'll be pleased to know you're all right. He was very worried about you. We all were."

She listened with growing concern. It seemed likely that Stan had deliberately gone away because he didn't want to face her and answer any awkward questions.

She said, "What about his wife? Is she away with him?"

Helen shook her head. "No. She's away but not with Stan. They had a quarrel about that Rosalie."

"Her cousin?"

"Yes. As much like Jean as a sister. A really brassy type. Jean sent her away and then left in a huff herself. She often does that. If we'd known we'd have insisted Stan attend the anniversary party. But with the bad feeling between Jean and the family we couldn't invite them both. I don't know how it's going to end."

Beth listened to all this and she had a vivid recollection of the blonde girl being struck down and Stan turning to her and saying that this was the way it had to end. It all seemed to fit so well and yet perhaps it had all been a fantasy in her mind induced by the fever. The whole episode might have been triggered by the appearance of Stan. From that instant she could have been in a state of collapse and the drama she'd seen enacted might have taken place in her sick mind.

She said, "It's too bad."

"Yes, it is," Helen agreed. "Now I mustn't stay any longer but one of us will be back to see you soon again."

The girl left and a thoroughly exhausted Beth closed her

eyes and slept. When she wakened in the early evening she felt a great deal better. She was able to sit up and take some light food. That night she rested well again and the following afternoon she was able to get out of bed and sit in a chair by the window of the hospital room.

She was seated there when Helen came again. "You are looking a lot better!" her friend said as she came in and took a chair opposite her.

"I feel almost myself again," she said.

"You mustn't try to rush things," Helen warned her.

"I'm not fond of hospitals. It was so stupid of me to have this spell," Beth lamented.

"Not at all. You couldn't help it."

"I knew about the risk but I didn't think it would happen."

Helen said, "Likely it will never happen again."

"I hope not."

"The family send you their best wishes," Helen said. "Alex was going to drop by last night but something came up and he couldn't. He asked to be remembered."

"Thank him for me," she said. Secretly she was glad the cynical Alex hadn't shown up as he might have sensed her upset state of mind.

Helen went on, "Mother and Father also asked about you. I hope you can soon return to the house and get a proper rest."

Beth kept an embarrassed silence for a moment and then she came to a decision. She felt she must tell her friend about the fantasy which was troubling her so. It might be a risk but she had to take it.

She began by saying, "There's something I must tell you about the night I became ill."

Helen appeared interested. "Yes?"

"I don't know how to begin," she faltered. "I was in bed

trying to read a mystery novel I found in the library when I was sure I heard a woman's scream above the storm."

Her friend stared at her. "A woman's scream?"

"Yes. Because I was ill I thought I'd imagined it. Then I heard it again and in spite of feeling so badly I decided to go downstairs and see if anything was wrong."

"And?"

Beth hesitated. "I was very weak and my head was reeling. I barely made it down to the lower landing. Then there was another scream and a pretty blonde woman came running into the room, obviously trying to escape from someone. And a few seconds later Stan came into the room after her. They were quarreling and hurled angry words at each other without paying the slightest attention to me. I guessed that the blonde girl must be Stan's wife."

Helen was staring at her incredulously. In a taut voice, she said, "Please go on."

Her cheeks were warm with embarrassment. She said, "I stood there, too ill to say or do anything. The quarrel became worse and then Stan picked up a silver candlestick from the table by the foot of the stairs and struck the blonde girl with it. She fell with blood streaming from her temple. I finally managed to call out to him. He gave me a strange look and said that it was the way things had to end between them. Then I collapsed."

There was a moment of tense silence in the hospital room as Beth finished her account. Helen was still staring at her in that odd fashion. Then the other girl said, "That really is a weird story."

"It was very real to me. All of it!"

"I can tell that by the way you repeat it."

Beth said, "When I came to here it was the first thing that I remembered. I was fully prepared to have some of the hospital people tell that Stan had killed his wife and turned himself in."

"You really expected that?"

"Yes."

"But it was all in your mind," Helen protested. "Part of your fever."

"I suppose so," she said lamely. "And yet it haunts me. It is exactly as if it happened."

"You mean you'll go on believing that it happened?"

"It will take me a while to get over it," Beth admitted.

Helen looked sympathetic. "But it had to be a fever nightmare. Stan did arrive at the house but you'd already collapsed. And as for Jean being there, that was impossible. She'd already left the area. So it had to be a fantasy on your part."

"I suppose so," she sighed. And she gave the other girl a questioning look. "But why that particular dream? Why would I picture Stan attacking his wife?"

"You've heard that they are unhappy in their marriage."

"That's true."

Helen suddenly showed new interest. "What about the mystery novel you were reading? Would that have suggested your fever dream?"

She frowned. "I don't know. I can't remember much about the book. I forced myself to read but I was so ill most of it escaped me."

Helen revealed a triumphant smile. "It so happens that I made up my mind to bring you something to read, and I thought you might want to finish the book you had in your bedroom. So I brought it along." She opened her handbag and brought out a blue-covered mystery novel. "There you are."

Beth took the novel and then found herself staring at the

cover in great excitement. For pictured there in the illustration under the title was the lovely blonde girl she'd seen murdered in her fantasy.

Pointing to the illustration, she exclaimed, "That's the girl! The one I saw!"

Helen spread her hands. "Then the mystery is solved. That explains everything. You had this girl's image in your mind and when you had the fantasy she became part of it."

Beth sat back in her chair feeling a great surge of relief. It was so logical it had to be the explanation. She had been a fool to think Stan had committed a murder and somehow managed to conceal it. She had suffered from a bad nightmare and that was all!

She said, "You don't know how relieved I am to find this out. I was really worried."

Helen smiled sympathetically. "I'm only thankful that I decided to bring the book along."

"It has made all the difference," she agreed, staring at the illustration featuring the blonde girl again. "Forgive me for being so foolish."

"Don't apologize," her friend said. "It might have happened. Heaven only knows Jean has given Stan reason enough to murder her. We think she's away with that Harvey Richard she's been carrying on an affair with. He's out of town as well. Of course everyone is gossiping about it. I feel worse for Mother than anyone else. Family means so much to her."

"Stan should divorce Jean," she said.

"I'm sure he will," Helen agreed. "It's partly stubbornness on his part. He married her against the wishes of all the family and he hates to admit that he was wrong and we were right."

"So he tortures himself."

"That's it. When he returns this time I'm going to have a serious talk with him," Helen said. "I'll try and persuade him to get a divorce at once. He can find grounds easily enough."

"I'm sure it would be the best thing," she said.

Helen told her, "He should have married you."

"I wouldn't say that," Beth protested. "He really doesn't know me that well. Nor do I know him. We got along well when we met in Africa but we spent only a short time together."

"He likes you. I can tell that," Helen said.

"Please don't tell him about my nightmare," Beth said. "I'd feel badly if I thought he'd heard about it."

"It will be our secret," Helen promised. "I'll not repeat a word of it to anyone."

Beth gave her a grateful smile. "I'm lucky to have a friend like you."

"Think nothing of it," Helen said briskly. And she reached into her handbag again. "I have a letter for you. It's probably from your father."

"I haven't heard from him in quite a while," Beth said as her friend passed her the airmail letter. Helen stood up. "Now I'll go and give you some privacy to read it. How soon before they'll release you?"

"Probably a day or two from now," she said. "I can go to a hotel in Boston. I don't feel like imposing on your family again."

"We wouldn't think of it," Helen said. "We're all looking forward to your return. I'll be here to drive you."

With that Helen left and Beth settled down to reading her letter. It was from her father and told about a new project he was working on in an area a hundred miles from the village where he made his home. It was full of details and had references to many people she knew so that it made her a little homesick.

When she finished the letter she put it aside and debated how she would answer it. She hated to worry her father but knew she should tell him of the recurrence of her fever. She was also worried about returning to the Moore mansion. In spite of having had the mystery of her nightmare explained, she still felt a reluctance to return to the old house. It was probably nonsense on her part but the events of that fevered dream still held a shocking reality for her.

Staring out the hospital window at the distant ocean, she had concerned thoughts about Stan Moore and his marital problems. Although she'd been reluctant to admit it to his sister, she had developed a true fondness for the intense dark young man. She much preferred him to the dour Alex and felt that he had borne up very well to the distress Jean had caused him.

At the moment there was little she could do but sympathize with him. He was a married man and unless he took definite steps he would go on being humiliated by the unfaithful Jean. She hadn't met the girl so she couldn't offer any personal judgment on her. But from what she'd heard from everyone else the ex-model was no suitable wife for Stan or anyone else. It was too bad.

It was strange how she'd put everything together in her dream. But the fact that the girl she'd seen struck by the candlestick had been the girl on the cover of the mystery novel seemed to settle the whole question. No matter how real it all seemed to her, it had been sheer fantasy. She had to make herself believe that.

She tried very hard to do this. Perhaps she tried too hard. For that night she suffered from tormenting dreams in which the scene in the living room came to her again and again. It was mixed up with her other nightmare of running through the forest seeking someone. And as usual she was left sobbing and alone.

Morning found her feeling the results of her troubled sleep. The doctor visited her and commented on her pale, drawn look but she didn't dare tell him about her nightmares. She faced the day with uneasiness. She had a feeling of apprehension, as if something dire were going to happen. And it turned out that her premonitions had some foundation.

Stan's mother arrived at the hospital in the late morning. The frail, aristocratic woman entered Beth's room with a look of concern on her pleasant face. Beth was standing in the middle of the room and the older woman came to her at once.

Andrea Moore said, "Helen was out when a message came for you. It is of so urgent a nature that I felt I should bring it to you without delay!"

Beth tensed at the woman's words. She at once felt it had to be bad news from Africa. In a low voice, she said, "Yes?"

"It's a cable from Africa," Andrea Moore said. "You'd better read it for yourself."

She took the cablegram and somehow managed to read it. It was almost what she'd expected. There had been an accident at the construction site and her father was injured. The cable stressed that while the injury was serious it need not be fatal. Her eyes blurred with tears as she put the message down.

Andrea Moore placed a comforting arm around her. "There, there my dear. It isn't all that bad. Judging by the message I'd say your father is in no danger."

"I must go back!"

"Are you well enough to go?"

"Yes. I have to be with him. I can't stay here while he's badly hurt and perhaps dying."

"You must do what you think best," Stan's mother said.

"But you also should listen to whatever advice the doctors here give you."

"I'll be all right," she insisted, thinking only of her father's plight.

Within an hour she'd talked with the hospital doctor and had won his reluctant approval to leave the hospital and take a limousine to the Boston airport. From there she'd take a flight to London and then a connecting flight to Capetown and finally on to Botswana. It would take her three days to reach her father's side following this tight schedule.

She did not need the limousine. Helen arrived at the hospital in her car before Beth was fully packed. Her friend helped her and then took her bags down to the car.

When they were both in the car and on the way to Boston Beth turned to the girl at the wheel and said, "You shouldn't have done this. I could have hired a limousine."

"Father and Mother would have been upset if you had," Helen told her. "Not to mention Stan. And anyway I still had one of your bags at the house. Now you have everything together. But I'm worried about your returning to Africa when you're still not well."

"I'm well enough," she insisted, though she was actually very weak.

"You must let us know how you make out and how your father is," Helen said.

"I will."

"Stan will be back in a few days and he'll be very upset at having missed you."

"Say goodbye to him for me," she asked.

Her eyes on the road, the girl at the wheel smiled wryly. "I will. But it will be a poor substitute for your doing it personally."

"I'll write him," Beth said.

"Please do," Stan's sister said.

They reached the Logan International Airport and Helen went with her to the BOAC lobby to get her baggage checked and her ticket. When that was done the two had coffee at a snack bar as Beth waited for her plane to leave.

Helen gave her a worried look. "You know I can't seem to get that fantasy you told me about out of my mind."

"I'm sorry I bothered you with it."

"No. You did the right thing. But it makes me wonder."

"Wonder what?"

Helen didn't reply for a moment. Then staring thoughtfully at her coffee cup, she said, "I've been wondering if your fantasy mightn't be a glimpse into the future, and it terrifies me."

Her eyebrows raised. "You think I might have foreseen something that will happen?"

The other girl gave her a solemn glance. "Yes."

"But now you're being ridiculous," she protested. "You know that the girl I saw in my nightmare was the same one whose likeness was on the cover of that mystery novel."

"I know."

"So that should settle it. I had a silly dream. You shouldn't let it worry you."

Helen gave her a knowing look. "It bothered you. I think maybe it still does."

"Not really," she protested, knowing this wasn't completely the truth but worried that she had upset Stan's sister.

"I'll try not to think about it," Helen promised. "I wish Stan would return. And Jean as well. Then maybe they'd get the trouble between them settled. They have to decide on a divorce."

"It has to be their decision," she pointed out.

"I know," Helen said with a sigh.

Beth's plane was announced and she said a hasty goodbye to Helen and went out to board it. Not too many minutes later the plane taxied out on the airstrip and she was starting the long journey to her father's side. She couldn't help but think of the friends she was leaving behind her in America and particularly of Stan.

She was probably in love with him. She'd felt drawn to him from their first meeting in Africa. Her reunion with him in America had made it plain that he felt the same way about her. But the unhappy marriage he'd made in the meantime was the stumbling block to any future for them. Perhaps while she was away he would decide to divorce Jean. It seemed the only hope.

Now that she was on her way back to Africa she regretted that she'd not at least had a passing glimpse of the girl Stan had married. She'd heard a great deal of talk about her and even driven by the house which Stan had bought for her, but Jean had never been in evidence.

So she had no idea what the girl who had come between herself and Stan looked like other than that she was a beauty and blonde. Helen had claimed that Jean's visiting cousin, Rosalie, had also had a striking resemblance to Stan's wife. But Beth had not seen Rosalie either.

Firmly she decided to put her recent experience out of her mind and concentrate on her reunion with her father.

Chapter Four

She arrived at London in the morning. There was a wait of three hours before she embarked on the plane for Capetown. And it was the twilight of still another day before a smaller plane landed her in Botswana. She was met by an associate of her father's, an elderly, gray-haired man who drove her in a jeep to the hospital.

She entered her father's room to find him apparently asleep with the wizened, old black housekeeper hunched in a chair by his bedside. The old woman rose with quick respect at her entrance.

Beth went close to her father and he stirred and opened his eyes. Seeing her, a smile came to his gaunt face. "I'm here, Father," she said.

He reached up a thin hand to take hers. "There was no need to come. I'm doing very well."

"I had to be here," she told him. And she bent down and kissed him.

They talked for the better part of a half-hour. Then the nurse came and suggested that she leave. Beth said goodnight to her father and left him.

She went out into the corridor which was now almost in darkness and saw that the ancient housekeeper had gone out there to wait for her. The old woman's bent figure came out of the shadows toward her.

"I wondered where you'd gone," Beth said.

The old woman gazed up at her, and in a weird voice intoned, "The curse is still with you."

"What are you talking about?" Beth gasped.

"The curse," the old woman hissed. "I can smell death around you."

She was shocked. "Are you saying that my father is going to die?"

The old woman shook her head. "No. This is death from a distant place. A place I have not seen. Someone has killed and you have seen the killing!"

Staring at the earnest face of the wizened woman in the shadows of the hospital corridor, Beth felt her heart pounding wildly. But she didn't want the ancient housekeeper to realize that she had frightened her with her weird pronouncement. That would not do.

She said sternly, "That was a wicked and stupid thing for you to say!"

"Yes, miss," the old woman said sullenly.

"Why did you say it?"

"Because of the voodoo! I can see what cannot be seen by others! I can tell of the secret things."

Beth was frightened by the old woman's reference to a distant murder in another land. It fitted in all too well with the strange fever dream she'd had and with Helen's apprehensions that the dream might become fact.

She said, "What can voodoo have to do with me?"

"You came down with the fever. It was the curse," the old woman vowed solemnly. "Now your father has been struck down. The curse has worked against him."

"My father had an accident! " Beth protested.

The old woman gazed up at her from the darkness and said, "He changed the course of the river and the jungle was flooded and now you both must suffer! The voodoo hand is set against you!"

"You are an ignorant and superstitious old woman," Beth told her angrily. "I will not have you in our employ any longer. Get your things at the house and I will pay you your salary. I want you to leave at once."

"Yes, miss," the old woman said without expression and she hobbled off down the dark corridor.

Beth watched her go with a feeling of dismay. The old woman had worked for her father for many years. She was not sure that he would understand or approve of her dismissing her. But under the circumstances she did not know what else she could do. It was not pleasant to be threatened by the strange old woman and have her say the frightening things she'd just said.

Beth went down to the waiting jeep and her father's associate began driving her back to the house. She sat very still and silent in the darkness as the jeep made its way over the bumpy road. Her return to Africa had not been a pleasant one.

The elderly engineer at the jeep's wheel asked her, "How did you find your father?"

She said, "He seemed in good spirits, but I still haven't any real idea of what is wrong with him."

"He fell. And I can't understand it. He's always been so very careful and sure-footed. I was there when it happened and I can't explain it. Neither can he. He claims it was almost as if some unseen force pushed him off the high girder."

She experienced a chill at the man's words. And she thought of the ancient black woman so solemnly stating that it was the curse which had caused her illness and her father's fall.

She said, "How badly hurt is he?"

"It's his back," the man at the wheel said. "They doubt

69

that he will ever walk again."

"Oh!" she said, stunned by the news.

"It will mean the end of his career if it's true," the driver of the jeep said. "But then they may be wrong. They often are."

"We can hope so," she said. But she had the feeling they wouldn't be.

A month later her father left the hospital in a wheelchair. The doctors told her that he would remain an invalid. He seemed to have accepted his fate with resignation and continued to direct the completion of the project on which he'd been working from his home. Daily the other engineers came for consultation sessions. Beth knew that this contact with his work sustained him but she worried about his future when this project was completed.

She had hired a new housekeeper, a younger woman sent to them from the Mission, but she had the uneasy feeling that this quiet, young woman was as devout a believer in voodoo as her elderly predecessor had been. Beth was conscious of the way the young woman sometimes stared at her and of the silent manner in which she moved around the house.

She kept in touch with Helen Moore by writing regularly. And after about six months had passed she noted a reference in one of Helen's letters that Stan had returned to live with the family. She took this as an indication that he'd either started divorce proceedings against his errant wife or was about to do so.

Her father's condition began to deteriorate. He found it necessary to spend most of his time in bed. And, sadly, about a year after the accident he died in his sleep. He was buried in the remote African village where he'd last worked, and Beth began packing to leave.

She'd had no recurrence of her fever since returning to Africa and her physical health was good. But mentally she was something of a wreck. The ordeal of her father's illness, her growing fear of the voodoo influences all around her, and her concern about her own future all took their toll.

Often she would waken in the middle of the hot African night to hear the weird throb of distant drums. She knew too well that they were probably beating out voodoo messages venomously directed against the white intruders in this new country.

Her father had given his whole life to projects to help backward countries, and yet it was whispered that he had died because he had challenged the voodoo power. And Beth knew that the natives in her household considered the curse was now on her.

She still had nightmares. But in them now she saw angry black faces and when she fled through the jungle in the horror of her dreams she was pursued by phantom figures wearing voodoo masks. She knew if she remained in Africa much longer she might have a complete breakdown. But where could she go?

She decided to spend a quiet month with her aunt in Bermuda and then go on to New York or Boston in search of work. And this was what she finally did. Much rested from her stay in Bermuda, she moved to Boston and found a position there as secretary to the director of an art museum.

The work was pleasant and she began to make some friends and have a social life of sorts. She found a small but charming apartment on Beacon Street and gradually the terrors in her past began to fade and become only vague memories.

It was on an evening in early May that she attended a crowded cocktail party at a friend's apartment in her building. She was standing talking to an elderly artist whom she'd met, when Helen Moore suddenly came up to her with a delighted smile.

"How good to see you!" Helen exclaimed. "I didn't know you were here in Boston! But then I haven't heard from you for months!"

"I'm sorry," she said, turning to the pretty brunette girl. "I've been on the move. And I've only recently settled here. I have intended getting in touch with you."

"I should hope so!" Helen said. "We often talk about you at home."

"How is everyone?"

"About the same. We were saddened by your father's death."

"It was a shock to me, though I was prepared for the possibility."

Helen said, "I'm glad you're back here." And she flashed a large engagement ring and wedding ring for her to see. "I married Ted Allan about a month ago."

"Congratulations," she said. "He's the fellow you were engaged to?"

"Yes," Helen nodded. "We're living in Marblehead only a street away from my parents' place. Ted was coming here tonight but he had to go to Chicago on business. You've never met him, have you?"

"No," she said. "I never have." She was remembering what she'd heard about the young man and was sure that Alex had spoken of him as drinking too much.

"You will," Helen said. "And you must get together with Stan. He has his office here in Boston, you know."

"How is he?" she asked. She didn't like to bring up the subject of whether he'd gotten his divorce or not, but she was curious.

"Much happier now that he's free," Helen replied, answering her question, though giving no details. "He'll be thrilled to know you are here in Boston. You remember how fond he is of you."

Beth felt her cheeks warm at this reference to her close friendship with the girl's brother. She said, "I always enjoyed his company."

Helen smiled warmly. "I'll phone him when I leave here tonight and tell him we met."

Anxious to change the subject, she asked about Helen's other brother. "How is Alex?"

"Still going his own way and as dour as usual," Helen said. "He spends less and less time in Marblehead. He has a group of his own friends in Cambridge and I think he prefers it there. Once in a while he comes home for a family party or an occasional weekend."

"I can see that he might prefer that freedom," she said.

"He's my brother, but I have never been able to feel close to him," Helen confessed.

"And your father and mother are well?"

"Father is well and busy. Mother worries me a little."

Beth showed concern. "In what way?"

"She's suddenly aged more than she should have and she seems nervous and frail," Helen said. "I try to stop by the house and see her at least once a day. I don't think she has enough outside life. And she frets too much about everything."

"I must get to Marblehead and your parents," she said.

You must visit us all," Helen insisted. "You're looking so well. So much better than when you were here before."

She smiled wryly. "I'd just recovered from my fever bout then."

"And you collapsed that stormy night of the anniversary

73

party," Helen recalled. "You've had no more spells like that?"

"No."

Helen gave her a significant look. "And you've had no more bad dreams like the one you had about Stan and Jean that night?"

Her cheeks warmed again. She said, "No. I seemed to lose my wild dreams with the fever."

"I'm glad," Helen said. "You were quite ill."

"Yes, I was."

Helen smiled again. "This has been wonderful. I'd like to spend the rest of the evening with you, but I have to meet Ted at the airport and then we'll be driving home. But I do want to see you soon."

"I'll be visiting Marblehead," Beth promised.

"And I am going to phone Stan," she said with a twinkle in her eyes and then vanished among the cocktail party crowd.

The meeting made a deep impression on Beth. And she realized that she'd not tried to get in touch with the Moore family because she'd not been certain she was ready to meet them again. That odd fantasy she'd had still haunted her and made her uneasy with them. It had been simple enough to write Helen an occasional letter, but renewing her friendship with the family was another matter. And especially renewing her friendship with Stan.

She was no longer certain how she felt about that young man. She almost hoped that Helen didn't tell him about her being in Boston, at least not for a while. She still didn't want to do much but be by herself or with strangers whom she'd not known in the past. She felt easier with new people. Finding herself involved in the affairs of the Moore family again might turn out to be a dubious pleasure.

The next day in the routine of her work she almost forgot the whole thing. But she'd barely entered her apartment that evening when the phone rang. She hastily picked up the phone without thinking and then heard Stan's familiar voice on the line.

"Hello, Beth," he said. "I want to see you."

"Stan," she said, caught between surprise and pleasure. "So Helen did tell you we met."

"Yes. And I can't understand why you haven't tried to get in touch with some of us before this," he said.

"I haven't been in Boston all that long," she said. "And I've been trying to find myself. This is a new life for me."

"I'd like to be part of it," Stan said.

"I do want to see you one day."

"That's far too vague. I refuse to wait," Stan said with all his old impetuosity. "Meet me for dinner tonight."

Beth hesitated. "I don't think so."

"Please," he said. "I've so many things to tell you. Can you meet me at the 57 Steak House in a half-hour?"

"I suppose so," she said. "But I'm not sure I should."

"Don't make me beg," he said unhappily. "I thought we were friends."

"I am your friend," she said, still reluctant to have this meeting so soon but not quite knowing how to get out of it.

"Then meet me at 57 around seven," Stan said. "I'll be waiting in the entrance for you."

Knowing how insistent he could be, she decided it was useless to protest further. With a small sigh, she said, "All right."

She had a hasty shower and changed into an attractive two-piece orange and white suit which she'd just bought and took a taxi to the downtown restaurant. Her feelings were mixed as she sat back for the taxi ride. She would try to keep things on a very platonic level with the young man until she'd made up her mind about him.

It was odd that a dream, or rather a fever fantasy, should so influence her that she hesitated meeting him again. But it was so. She couldn't have been more hesitant about it if the incident had really happened. Perhaps it was silly of her, but she couldn't help it.

Still, when she left the taxi and made her way into the big restaurant she felt a thrill of excitement at seeing the handsome Stan waiting there for her. He was wearing a brown suit and he looked much less care-worn than when she'd last seen him.

Coming to greet her with a smile, he took her hand in his and kissed her on the cheek. "You look marvelous!" was his warm comment.

The headwaiter led them to a table by a raised pool of water in the center of the ornate restaurant with its walnut paneled walls hung with fine old paintings.

She looked around her as she sat down and with a smile said, "This is an interesting combination of the old and the new. I like it."

"I'm glad you approve," he said, studying her across the table. "You don't know how I've longed to see you."

She gave him a look of wry amusement. "I've missed you."

"But you weren't going to get in touch with me," he reproved her. "If Helen hadn't met you by accident, we'd never have heard from you."

She knew this might well be true but to admit it would be too awkward. So she said, "No. I would have gotten in touch after a while."

"Why the delay?"

She looked down at the table top to avoid his questioning eyes. "Several reasons," she said. "I've just emerged from a shattering experience. I've been trying to find myself."

"You mean your father's death," he said. "I'm sorry about that. He was a fine man."

"I thought so," she said quietly.

"But that isn't a good enough reason for you to shut yourself away from all your old friends," he argued.

"There were other things," she said. "My state of health. I had that strange fever. I wanted to be sure I was over it. Africa is a bizarre place. The old woman who looked after our house blamed my father's death and my fever on a voodoo curse. For a time I began to wonder if she weren't right."

Stan's handsome face registered surprise. "You actually thought that? That you and your father might be victims of voodoo?"

"Yes. So you see I'm a more primitive creature than you guessed," she said with a rueful smile.

"I can understand your feelings," he said. "Those things taking place the way they did and you in that remote country. But you're in Boston. No voodoo curse is going to follow you here."

"They're very potent, I understand. Don't underestimate the chances," she said.

"Consider the curse destroyed by our meeting," he said with a smile of encouragement. "Last time I saw you it was the night of that bad storm."

The mention of the night made her nervous. "Yes," she said in a small voice.

"I came into the house thinking my parents might have returned," he said. "And instead I saw you standing on the landing in a dazed state. And in the next moment you collapsed."

She said, "I must have seen you before I blacked out."

It seemed to her that for just a second he hesitated and

looked uncertain. Then he quickly said, "Yes. I went over and saw your condition and phoned for an ambulance."

"I don't remember anything until I woke up in the hospital days later," she said.

"By that time I had been called away on business," Stan said. "Then the word came about your father's accident and you left this country before I had a chance to see you again."

"I know," she said. And it troubled her that she still found his account of events that night so hard to believe. The fantasy she'd experienced had made such a deep impression on her. She could even now see him rushing into the living room in pursuit of the blonde beauty and the violence which had followed.

The waiter came and took their orders and for a while they chatted politely about Helen's marriage and the fact that Alex had taken up more-or-less permanent residence in Cambridge. Then over coffee the mood between them became more intimate.

With a knowing look, he said, "You know that I'm free now."

She nodded. "Helen told me. When did you divorce Jean?"

His handsome face shadowed. "She didn't tell you any of the details then?"

"No."

Rather awkwardly he said, "There was no divorce."

She said, "I don't understand."

Stan's face was gaunt. "You knew we weren't getting along?"

"Yes."

"Just about the time you were at my parents' house Jean had her cousin, Rosalie, visiting us. She created problems

78

and I told Jean she had to go. Jean sent her away but there was a bitter quarrel between us about it. One of many, I might say."

"Then what?"

"I made it clear to Jean that I meant to divorce her no matter what. She'd been carrying on with our neighbor Harvey Richard among others and I had all the evidence I needed to get my freedom."

"What was her reaction?"

"I think she knew there had to be a showdown," Stan said with a frown. "Maybe she was prepared for it. She warned me that she could make it costly for me. And then she taunted me by telling me that Harvey would be delighted to marry her. She was pretty, you know, and so was that Rosalie. They could have been sisters and their characters were a lot alike. Rosalie even made a play for Harvey when she was our guest. I think that convinced Jean to send her away more than my demanding it."

"So?"

"Jean vanished. Harvey Richard went away at the same time. I assumed they were together. I no longer cared. I went to New York on business and when I returned she still hadn't showed up. I was sure she was with Harvey Richards by that time."

"But she wasn't?" Beth suggested.

Stan frowned. "No. Richards returned and I became upset. I went to his place and challenged him about Jean and where she was. He said he'd gone away alone and he had no idea where Jean was."

She stared at him. "What then?"

"I was in a panic."

"What did you do?"

"I notified the police she was missing. Tried to locate her

cousin at the Boston address she'd given us. But she was no longer there. I waited to see if the police could find Jean."

"Did they?"

"Yes," he said, his handsome face solemn. "They found her about a month later."

"Where?"

"On a beach about two miles from Marblehead. The swift tides had carried her body there."

Beth was shocked. So Jean was dead. The attractive girl whom she'd never met and yet who had played a fairly important part in her life had died without their paths ever crossing.

She said, "What happened?"

He looked grim. "The police put it down as suicide. They claim she must have thrown herself over the cliffs by our place and then the sea carried the body along down the beach."

"Why?"

"I think after we had our showdown she must have gone to Harvey and told him about it," was Stan's reply.

"And?"

"Harvey is the middle-aged playboy type. He would want no part of marriage with Jean. He probably told her so. They must have had a quarrel and in her upset state she decided to kill herself. He left, not knowing what he'd driven her to. He seemed as surprised by her suicide as I was."

She gave him a searching look. "Do you really think Jean killed herself? From all I've heard she was hardly the type for that."

"I've asked myself that question," he admitted.

"And?"

"I can only think of one other possibility."

"What?"

"Harvey might have thrown her over the cliffs after he

tired of her, knowing she was going to try and force him into marriage."

"Is he that violent a person?"

"I'd say no," Stan said. "His weakness is women. He's had some strange girl living there with him lately. She comes and goes. I've had a glimpse of them in his car. She's dark and usually wears blue glasses."

Beth said, "Did you sell your house when you moved back in with your parents?"

"No," he said. "I've closed it up and removed everything of Jean's. There's nothing there to remind me of her now. But I still couldn't face living there alone."

"I don't blame you."

Stan sighed. "It was a bad business from start to finish."

"At least it's over."

"Yes. It's over," he agreed. "Much as I had come to despise Jean I still grieve over her death."

"I know," she said.

He offered her a twisted smile. "So you see you haven't been the only one who's been having a bad time."

"I realize that," she said.

"One of my reasons for wanting to see you was to explain all this," Stan said.

"I have wondered," she admitted. "Naturally I assumed you had divorced Jean."

"Now you know," he said.

"I hope things will be better for you in the future," Beth told him.

He eyed her across the table significantly. "You have something to say about that."

"Oh?"

"I'm very lonely," he said. "I need company. And I enjoy your company."

81

Beth said, "There must be lots of other girls anxious to go out with you."

"But I'm not all that interested in going out with them," Stan said. "I made a mistake once. I don't want to risk repeating it."

Beth studied him with sympathy. "I've already told you I'm not in any mood for a serious affair."

"You told me once you were in love with me."

"I said I liked you," she protested. "And I still do."

"Then let us go on seeing each other," he insisted.

"We can meet once in a while."

"It has to be more than that," Stan said. "I need you too badly."

"I can't promise anything more."

He picked up his check and said, "I'll settle this and we can move across to the lounge. They have a trio there who play very well."

"I should be going home," she said.

"But it's still early," he protested and he hailed the waiter to settle his check.

They transferred to the lounge where an organist, a bass player and a drummer provided suitably pleasant music. The room was nearly as large as the main restaurant and well decorated. The light was soft-key and there were small comfortable sofas for sitting. They found a vacant one and Stan ordered drinks. After a moment he left her to make a business phone call he'd forgotten to take care of earlier.

Beth sat alone listening to the music. She had her drink and pocketbook on the coffee table in front of her. All at once a stranger appeared and reached down to take her pocketbook.

She looked into his face with frightened eyes until she

saw that it was Alex Moore, Stan's dour brother. The young man with the horn-rimmed glasses offered her a malicious smile.

"Did I scare you?" he asked.

"You know you did," she told him reprovingly.

He sat by her. "I was at the bar with a friend. I saw you come in with my respected brother."

"Yes. He's making a phone call."

"Good," Alex said in his mocking way. "It gives me a chance to talk to you."

"You're still as incorrigible as ever!" she accused him.

"I'm not a bit more popular with the family than before," he was willing to admit. "They don't see as much of me these days."

"So I understand."

The eyes behind the heavy glasses fixed on her. "So you're seeing Stan again?"

"Yes. At least this is the first time we've been together since I've returned to Boston."

Alex said, "You want some good advice?"

She stared at him. "What sort of advice?"

"The best. Stay away from Stan."

She frowned. "Why do you say a thing like that about your brother?"

The young man with the horn-rimmed glasses looked pleased with himself. He said, "Because he is my brother. I know him better than you do."

"What does that mean?"

Alex shrugged. "I'd say it means the Moore family isn't a healthy group for you. Maybe not for anyone."

"You're talking nonsense," she chided him.

"I'm being honest with you," he said. "Think it over." And he got up.

She stared up at him. "Aren't you going to wait and see Stan?"

He shook his head. "No. He won't mind missing me."

"Why do you have to act so strangely?" she asked him.

"The family likes me this way," he said. "They like to think I'm the one who is strange." With a nod he left her and went back to the bar.

She watched and saw him pay for his drinks and then leave with another young man about his own age and build who also was wearing horn-rimmed glasses. She saw them go out the side exit and sat back on the love seat with a troubled expression on her pretty face.

Alex enjoyed being mysterious and saying wild things but he had outdone himself tonight. Why had he warned her against dating Stan? And why had he so bluntly said the Moore family might not be healthy for her? Did he know something he hadn't told her? Perhaps something about the strange fate of Stan's wife?

All her own doubts and suspicions came racing back as a result of her meeting Alex and the odd way he'd talked. She knew she shouldn't allow him to upset her and yet he had. Perhaps it was because she was vulnerable in this situation. She still had the weird memories of that stormy night to contend with.

But her fantasy that night had been no more than that. She'd drawn the blonde from the book cover and the situation from her too vivid imagination. Once Stan had shown her the candlestick and she'd thought what a lethal weapon it would make. And in her fever dream she'd included the candlestick in the imagined violence.

"You look very preoccupied," Stan said as he returned to sit beside her.

She made an effort to rouse herself from her troubled

84

mood. She said, "I was just speaking with your brother."

"Alex?" he sounded surprised.

"Yes."

"I didn't know he ever came in here."

"It's a public place and fairly central," she pointed out.

"Yes. That's true. Boston isn't all that large. You do run into people more often than you would in a bigger city. So he came over to see you?"

"Yes."

"Why didn't he wait for me?"

"He didn't seem all that anxious to talk to you," Beth said.

"That figures," Stan said with a grim smile showing on his lean, handsome face. "We don't get on all that well."

"Why?"

"I couldn't begin to explain. We fought as boys."

"And it still goes on."

"In a way. What did he say about me?"

"Nothing flattering."

"I know that."

"He warned me against you," she said, giving him a sharp study as she said it.

Stan again looked uncertain for perhaps a few seconds as if he didn't know how to answer her. Then he changed and smiling coldly said, "That was rather stupid of him."

"I thought so," she said. "I asked him what he meant."

"And?"

"He wouldn't explain," she said

Stan nodded. "He wouldn't explain because he couldn't. He saw a chance to try and cause trouble and took it. That's an old trick with him."

"Is it?" she asked him solemnly.

"You know it is," Stan said with some irritation. "Or do

you want to believe him, that I'm a dangerous character?"

"I don't want to believe him."

"Then let's not discuss it any further," her escort said. "Don't let it spoil our evening since that's clearly what he wants."

So they said no more about it. But it had cast a shadow over their enjoyment. She was aware of a certain reserve in Stan which he'd not showed before and she expected that she had also become somewhat more tense.

Stan saw her back to her apartment. They kissed goodnight but more in the manner of friends going through the polite motions than with the ardor of lovers. He made mention of calling her soon again and she accepted this quietly but without giving him any real encouragement.

That night for the first time in many months she dreamed again about being lost in the forest and seeking her mother. This time the familiar portion of the dream blacked out and she found herself once again on that landing on the night of the storm. And the whole drama of Stan pursuing the frightened blonde into the room and killing her with the candlestick was replayed in her mind. She awoke screaming and drenched with perspiration.

It terrified her! The nightmare had been so real! And she'd so clearly recalled every detail of the original. She sat up in bed staring into the darkness and worrying that it must mean something. The dream must have some message for her!

But when daylight came she told herself that her fears were silly and baseless. She'd let the darkness and a bad dream frighten her into thinking things which weren't true. She was little better than the natives with their belief in voodoo. Dreams were simply that and nothing more.

86

Chapter Five

Beth returned to her placid routine and almost forgot about the Moores. Yet she'd not completely forgotten Stan. Whenever the phone in her apartment rang in the evening, she went to answer it with the thought he might be calling. Oddly enough, he didn't. She found this puzzling since he'd seemed so anxious to see her again.

Then early one evening about two weeks after their dinner together as she sat curled up on the divan in her living room reading a book, her doorbell rang. As she seldom had any visitors she was nervous. She put down the book and slowly went over to the door and opened it on the safety chain. At once she was shocked for standing out there in the hall was Andrea Moore, Stan's mother.

The older woman was dressed in prim New England fashion in a tailored dark suit and a small round black hat with a tiny veil perched on her graying hair.

"May I come in?" she asked. "I have something urgent to discuss with you."

Gradually recovering from her nervousness, Beth opened the door and let Andrea Moore in. She said, "I have very few visitors and I always like to know who it is before I take off the chain."

"You're very wise," the older woman said. "It wasn't so long ago that the Boston Strangler was causing terror here."

"The landlord warned me to be careful," Beth said. And leading Stan's mother into the living room, she invited her,

"Please sit down."

"Thank you," Andrea Moore said with a wan smile on her thin, lined face. "I hope you won't think me too forward. But I happened to be in the city and since Helen told me you were here I have wanted to talk to you."

Beth sat in a plain chair opposite the older woman. She was trying not to show her surprise at seeing Stan's mother. "Would you care for a cup of tea or coffee?" she asked.

"No, nothing, thanks," Andrea Moore said. "You're very comfortable here."

"I like it," she said.

Andrea Moore said, "We were all so saddened by the news of your father's death."

Beth said, "I miss him a great deal."

"Of course you would be bound to," Stan's mother said. "You have heard about the suicide of Stan's wife, I'm sure."

"Yes."

The older woman gazed down at her folded, gloved hands and sighed. "A dreadful business. I never approved of her. But I was shocked by the way her life ended."

"You would be," Beth said. And she was thinking that for all the older woman's frail appearance there was a definite strength about her.

Stan's mother fixed anxious blue eyes on her and said, "That is one of the reasons for my being here. Jean's suicide has left Stanley in a very depressed state."

"I hadn't realized that."

"It is true. They didn't get on well. But he had cared for her once and it was distressing to have her take her own life. I think perhaps he may be harboring guilt feelings, though there is no reason that he should."

"I agree."

The older woman sighed. "I have had problems with all

my children. Helen has married Ted Allan, a nice enough young man but inclined to drink too much. We seem to have lost Alex to his friends in Cambridge and now Stanley is shadowed by tragedy."

Beth said, "I'm sure things are not as bad as they seem."

"That is what my husband tells me," Andrea Moore said. "But I worry and I wonder. I don't mind confessing that." She gave Beth a look of direct appeal. "And I believe you can help."

"In what way?"

"I happen to know that Stanley is very fond of you," Andrea Moore said. "I think you might bring him out of his terrible depression. If you would marry him, I'm sure you could save him."

Beth had hardly expected to hear such a frank statement. For a moment she was unable to reply. Then she said, "I like Stan but I haven't thought of marrying him and I very much doubt if he is interested in me in that way."

Stan's mother told her, "I can assure you that he is. He has discussed you with me. And I know how he feels about you. If he should call you, I hope you'll see him. He needs someone badly."

Embarrassed, she said, "No doubt we'll be seeing each other. And if I were you, I wouldn't worry too much about all this."

"I'll try not to," the older woman said with a smile. "Now I really must be going. My husband is waiting for me in the car."

"You should have had him come up with you," Beth said as she accompanied her to the door.

"No," Andrea Moore said. "Then I wouldn't have dared to speak so plainly. It was better for it to be just the two of us." She gave her a pleading look. "You will think about what I said, won't you?"

"I will," she said, though she knew it was something about which she would surely make up her own mind.

"Bless you!" the older woman said warmly and she kissed her on the cheek in parting.

Beth saw her to the stairway and then walked back to her apartment in an almost bewildered mood. It was a visit she'd never expected, nor had she expected such a strange request from the aristocratic Andrea Moore. She could imagine Stan's rage if he even guessed his mother had done anything like this. And she made up her mind not to ever mention it to him if he should call her again.

It was a strange business. Beth had almost forgotten about the visit by the time Stan phoned her a week later. He was very reserved in manner as he invited her to see a movie with him. She agreed to go and a time was arranged.

He met her at the apartment and they walked to the movie. It was a good one and they both enjoyed it. Afterward she invited him to her apartment for drinks.

Glass in hand, he sat on the end of the divan and smiled at her. He said, "I suppose you wondered why I've been so long in calling you again?"

She nodded. "I did wonder."

The young man said, "I was having an argument with myself. Fighting myself not to bother you. I'd made up my mind you didn't want my company and I battled myself to leave you alone."

Her eyes twinkled. "And you lost."

"Yes. I lost. I suppose that annoys you?"

"No," she smiled. "I'm really glad you lost. I did want to see you again."

Stan's handsome face brightened. "Then you've changed your mind about me?"

90

"I wouldn't say that," she told him. "I've merely decided it might be fun for us to go on seeing each other."

And so began a long series of dates. Stan asked her to marry him one night in mid-August. She agreed and they made plans to have a small and very private wedding in September. His only request of her was that she attend an announcement party at his parents' place. Since he presented it as a placating gesture for the older folk, she agreed.

On a Saturday in late August the party was held with all the immediate family in attendance. Dinner was served and later they went out on the lighted patio for drinks and conversation. Helen was there with her husband and Beth met him for the first time. Ted Allan was a big, sandy-haired man with a warm smile and the florid cheeks of a heavy drinker.

He took Beth off to a corner of the patio where they could talk freely without being overheard and in a confidential manner he told her, "Let me warn you, I was a close friend of Jean's."

His mention of Stan's dead wife came as a shock to her. She said, "I never did meet Jean."

"No?" The big man took a gulp of his drink.

"No," she said. "So I can't offer any personal opinion about her. I only know what others have said."

Ted winked at her drunkenly. "And the others have said plenty. I know that!"

"I don't pay much attention to gossip," she said.

"Wise young woman," Helen's husband said, his words just a trifle slurred to betray his heavy drinking. "Jean was all right."

She glanced away toward the bushes, not wanting to annoy him him but also anxious to have him end the conversation. She said, "I think I'll enjoy living here in Marblehead."

Ted's florid face showed an arrogant smile. "You're not as pretty as she was!"

"That's too bad," she said, trying to keep it light.

"You think you're going to be happy with him?" He nodded to where Stan was talking with his father.

"Why not?"

"You're going to live in her house?" Ted asked drunkenly.

"I'm going to live in the house Stan owns," she said. "He only closed it temporarily."

Ted was swaying slightly. "You been all through it?"

"No. I'm waiting until later. He has decorators in there doing it over. He doesn't want me to see it until it's ready."

"You won't like it," the big man taunted her.

"How do you know?" she challenged him.

"Jean's ghost," Helen's husband said with a sly smile. "You'll never have any peace from it in that house!"

She was stunned at his cruel humor. It was evident that he had been fond of Jean and so had decided to take a dislike to her. She said, "I have every reason to hope Stan and I will be very happy in the house!"

Helen came up to them with a nervous smile. "I heard that," she said. "And I'm sure you're right. Who suggested anything different?"

"I did," Ted told his wife drunkenly. "I'm on Jean's side!"

Helen gave him a concerned look. "You've been drinking too much and we're going home!"

"Oh! Oh!" the big man said in a childlike way. "I've done it again!" And he meekly allowed Helen to lead him from the patio.

Stan's mother came up to her with a nervous smile. She said, "I notice that Helen is taking Ted home. I hope he wasn't nasty to you."

"It was all right," she said, still some upset.

Andrea looked troubled. "He's not responsible when he's drinking. And that's most of the time. I warned Helen before they were married but she wouldn't listen. Now she is finding out for herself. What was he saying to you?"

"It seems he was a good friend of Jean's."

Stan's mother considered. "I believe he did know her."

"He was comparing us and I didn't measure up too well," Beth said with a bitter smile.

"Drunken nonsense!" Stan's mother said with disgust. "Please accept my apologies for his behavior."

"It didn't matter," she said. "Even a person like Jean is bound to have some champions. What I disliked is his conviction that Stan and I can't possibly be happy in that house."

"Pay no attention to his talk!" her future mother-in-law said angrily.

Beth didn't want to believe what the drunken man had said but once again something had touched on the chords of her memory to make her uneasy. The death of Stan's wife was cloaked in mystery. Unless new facts were discovered, it would never be certain whether she had been a suicide or a murder victim. The police had accepted the suicide theory because it settled the case at once. But clearly some people — Ted, for example — must have suspicions about her death.

Stan's father came over to them and said, "It seems I hardly ever get a minute alone with you, Beth."

His wife smiled and told him, "Well, have one now." And. with a warm nod for Beth she walked away from them.

Stephen Moore watched his wife go and then told Beth, "You know you've done wonders for her."

"I'm not sure I follow you," Beth said.

His stern face showed a warm look as he explained. "After Jean's suicide my wife was very upset. She worried a great deal about the scandal, as she is family proud, and on another level she was very concerned about Stan and what the sad business might do to him. As soon as she heard you two were to be married she changed almost overnight. She's her old self again."

"I'm glad."

"It's a great burden off my mind," Stephen Moore confided. "I didn't know what might happen to her."

Beth said, "Do you think we're making any mistake by planning to live in that same house?"

The gray-haired man seemed surprised. "Why shouldn't you live there? It's a fine property and Stan spent a small fortune furnishing it."

"I agree," she said. "I'm sure it will work out well."

Later in the evening she found herself in the company of the mocking Alex. He had been persuaded by his mother to come to Marblehead for the party.

Stan's younger brother gave her a grim smile over his glass. "You don't pay attention to warnings, do you?"

She raised her eyebrows. "Do you mean what you said to me that night in the bar?"

"Yes. I told you to avoid Stan."

"You couldn't have expected me to take you seriously."

The eyes behind the horn-rimmed glasses were fixed on her as Alex said, "I hoped that you would. I see I was wrong."

"You gave me no reasons. I thought it was one of your offbeat jokes."

"You were very wrong," Alex said. "I hate to bring a sour note to this festive occasion but if I were you I'd run — and fast!"

Beth gave a mirthless laugh. "That's about the nicest thing anyone could say to a girl at her engagement party."

"I've told you the Moores are bad medicine for you."

"I can vouch for you," Beth said. "Why do you dislike me?

Are you another of Jean's secret admirers?"

This seemed to startle him. He asked, "Why did you ask that?"

It was her turn to assume a mocking air. "I think it's only fair to know where you stand," she said.

Alex gave her a cold glance. "I can promise you that you don't know where you stand," he said and he abruptly left her.

It was getting late and Stan came up to her and asked, "Was my kid brother annoying you again?"

"No more so than usual."

"Give me the word and I'll remove him by the scruff of the neck," her husband-to-be told her.

She smiled thinly. "That drastic action won't be necessary," she said. "I think it's about time you drove me back to Boston. It's getting late."

He glanced at his watch. "You're right. We'll say goodnight to my parents and get under way."

Ten minutes later they were heading back to Boston with Stan at the wheel. He gave her a glance in the semi-darkness of the front seat.

"You're suddenly very quiet," he said. "Didn't you enjoy the party?"

"Of course. I'm just a little weary."

"Mother went all out to make it a success," he said.

"Yes, I know," she sighed.

"What's wrong?" he asked.

"There was someone at the party making it difficult for me," she said.

"Who?" he asked sharply.

"Jean."

"Jean!" he repeated incredulously.

"Yes."

"What are you talking about?" he demanded as they drove along in the late night.

"It was her ghost. In the minds of all the others. She's still so fresh in their memory. I'll have to wait until she fades from their minds before they'll accept me."

His handsome profile showed concern. "I think you're very wrong," he said.

"No," she told him. "It's true. Even those who are happy about our marriage like your mother are still haunted by Jean's memory. It will take time to settle that ghost."

"You worry me when you talk this way," he complained.

"Don't worry," she said, moving close to him and resting her head against him. "It will be all right. I can wait and win out. I'm not afraid of Jean."

She really believed this. And it was this belief which carried her through the days that followed. In early September she and Stan drove to the Berkshires and were married in a country church with two strangers as witnesses and the only guests at the ceremony. While they were in the church a thunder and lightning storm darkened the skies and brought torrents of rain.

They made laughing references to "happy the bride the sun shines on" as they ran to their car. But in spite of her brave front, the storm made Beth suddenly frightened. It was so like that night when she'd had the fever spell and Stan had found her. She sat watching the forked lightning cross the sky and hearing the loud thunder as Stan drove further into the mountain country.

Then after a half-hour it cleared miraculously and left in its wake a golden rainbow. Her tension left her as she decided this had to be a good omen.

Seemingly it was. The balance of their week-long honeymoon was as wonderful as she had dreamed it would be. They stayed at several charming inns and had perfect weather. And by the time they headed back to Marblehead she was convinced she and Stan would have a long and blissful marriage.

It was late on a moonlit night when they reached the stately white colonial house on the cliff overlooking Marblehead harbor. She made her first entrance into the newly decorated house with faint blue beams of moonlight streaming in through the windows. She stood for a moment in the semi-darkness and knew her first moment of misgivings in the week since her marriage.

She could almost sense a chill, ghostly presence in the house! Then Stan followed her in and jovially said, "What's the idea standing there in the dark?" And he switched on the lights, flooding the area.

Feeling less tense in the lighted room, she managed a smile as she turned to him. She said, "It is a lovely house. I'm glad I waited until now to see it."

"And you shall see it all!" Stan said happily. And after he'd brought in her bags he gave her a complete tour of the house, turning on the lights from cellar to attic.

Beth laughed. "What will people think?"

"They'll know we're home and inspecting our property," he said.

When they'd finished the tour they had a snack in the kitchen before going upstairs to bed. As he turned out the lights at the bottom of the stairs, Stan took her in his arms.

"No regrets?" he asked.

She smiled up at him. "No regrets," she said softly.

He kissed her gently and she relaxed completely in his arms.

But her moment of relaxation was to be brief, for at that same instant an eerie droning rose directly behind her. She started nervously at the sound.

Stan said, "It's the grandfather clock. It's over there." He indicated a corner lost in the shadows.

She listened as the old clock chimed seven times and then stopped. Looking up at him, she said, "It only chimed seven and it must be midnight."

"Don't let it bother you," Stan told her. "I'll take care of it in the morning. There has been no one in the house to keep it regulated."

She started up the stairs with him, making no reply. But the weird interruption of the clock had made her wonder if a ghostly hand mightn't have caused it to chime at that precise moment. It fitted in with her first impression of the old house.

Long after Stan was sleeping soundly she lay awake staring into the darkness and hearing strange creaks and sighs from the old place. And she was convinced there was something here she did not understand and which she could not cope with. She regretted that she had not insisted on Stan finding another house. Finally she slept.

In the morning with the sun flooding the airy rooms and with the magnificent view of the ocean offered from most of the windows, she couldn't do anything but enjoy her home.

When she was out in the garden she had her first glimpse of the neighbor in the cottage just beyond them. He was a tall, good-looking man of middle-age with a bronzed face and the slight hint of a stomach. He was standing on the patio behind the cottage in company with a slim dark-haired girl who wore black glasses. It was hard to tell what the girl looked like because of the glasses. After a moment the two went inside.

She told Stan about seeing the two when he joined her in

the garden. She said, "The girl seems much younger than him."

Stan gazed in the direction of the cottage grimly. He said, "That's Harvey Richard and his latest conquest."

She raised her eyebrows. "The Harvey Richard?"

"Who else?" her husband said irritably. "He's almost my father's age but he continues to act the bachelor playboy! He had both Jean and that Rosalie running after him! His conquests would make a roster of a good portion of the country club's female members."

Beth smiled, "I wonder you brought me here to live. What makes you think I'll be safe?"

"You've been warned," he said.

"I doubt if that's ever enough to keep someone from being attracted to a Harvey Richard," she said.

Stan gave her a strange look. "Then there's what happened to Jean to curb him."

"You think he feels guilt in her death?"

"He should."

"You talked to him after she vanished, didn't you?"

"Yes. He pretended innocence. To hear him tell it they'd hardly been friends, let alone lovers."

"But that wasn't true."

"It certainly wasn't," Stan said grimly.

"Perhaps he was merely trying to spare your feelings," she said.

"He's hardly noted for his kindness to husbands."

"Still," she said, "he knew you were very upset about what had happened to Jean."

Stan nodded. "And he was either responsible for her taking her own life or he shoved her over the cliff himself."

She took a deep breath. "You're saying we may be living next to a murderer?"

"It's very likely," her husband said in a taut voice.

She turned to study his troubled face. "But if Jean was everything you've said, isn't it possible she deliberately led him on?"

"Perhaps. He wouldn't need much encouragement."

"But in that case wouldn't she be the major offender?"

Stan frowned. "I haven't tried to apportion the blame."

"If she hadn't been carrying on an affair with Harvey Richards, it would probably have been with someone else, don't you think?"

"Very likely," he agreed with a sigh. "Why bring all this up?"

"Because if it is true you cannot fairly blame her suicide on him. Assuming she killed herself."

Her new husband stared at her. "You're saying she was the offender?"

"Yes. He probably went along with what seemed a good thing. That's a human enough reaction. But she was the aggressor. And if she cracked up emotionally in the end and threw herself from the cliff, it was as a result of her own actions."

"What if Richard decided she'd become a nuisance and, angered by her demands that he marry her, shoved her down to her death?"

"I don't think that happened."

Stan's handsome face showed annoyance. "How can you possibly know?"

"For one thing you'd only just told her you were going to divorce her. The divorce hadn't come about yet. So though she may have asked him to marry her, there was actually no crisis yet."

"I suppose not," Stan said reluctantly.

"It was obviously too soon to quarrel about their marriage

before Jean's marriage with you had been dissolved," she said.

"They could have quarreled about something else," he pointed out.

"True."

"Rosalie might have provided a reason," Stan went on.

"I told you that young cousin of Jean's made a definite play for our amorous neighbor."

"Did Jean and she have any words about it?"

"I'm almost sure they did."

"You've come up with an interesting possibility," she said. "But by that time Rosalie was no longer here. You'd made Jean send her away."

"And that was a grim business. Not that I think Jean wanted her here any longer, she had come to realize the girl was a threat where Harvey Richard was concerned."

"But she still made a scene about sending her away?"

Stan shrugged "Rosalie was her blood relative. Anything I said against her was taken very personally by Jean. Especially since I pointed out that they were a lot alike."

She smiled thinly. "Not flattering under the circumstances."

"Hardly."

Beth glanced beyond the hedges surrounding the garden toward the Richard cottage. It was not large in size but had been expensively constructed and showed it. The patio out back had tan brick walls part way to give privacy. She'd seen the girl and Harvey Richard standing on the far end of the patio beyond the walls and it was possible they were still outside but screened from view by the high barrier of white bricks. There was enough distance between the two houses so that voices could not be heard clearly enough to eavesdrop.

Beth glanced at her husband again. "When did Jean first

meet Harvey Richard?"

He furrowed his brow and stared at the distant cottage. "About a week after I first bought this place and we moved in here. Richard gave a small welcoming party for us. It was in July and he made a lot of it because it was Jean's birthday month. He takes an interest in astrology."

"Oh?"

"He talked about the Cancer sign being one of the most interesting and Jean ate it all up. He's always been a Sunday painter and has the cottage filled with astrological paintings. The next thing I knew he was making a painting of Jean, a portrait incorporating her astrology sign. That gave them an excuse for being together. She began spending more and more of her time over there."

She gave him a significant look. "You must have known what was going to happen? You knew Harvey Richard's reputation."

Stan looked glum. "The husband is always the last to guess. I knew he was a threat but I felt secure about Jean. I didn't think she'd ever let me down."

"But she did."

"She did. I later found out that faithfulness wasn't her thing. So in one way you're right. If it hadn't been Harvey Richard it would have been someone else."

"You can accept that now because you've become completely disillusioned about Jean. Even with her memory."

Her eyes met her husband's. "I wonder that you wanted to return here and live. The house must be haunted by Jean for you and you're constantly exposed to seeing Harvey Richard."

"That's why I redecorated and removed everything of hers," he said. "We're beginning fresh again. And as for Harvey, I think for the reasons I've mentioned he'll let us alone."

"I hope so," she said, glancing at the cottage with its imposing brick-walled back patio once again. For her own part she was still uneasy in this house where Stan had lived with his first wife. The fear she'd known in the night had faded to just a vague restlessness in the daylight. But somehow she felt that the spirit of a malevolent Jean remained in the house waiting to take revenge on her for usurping her position.

Stan's handsome face showed uncertainty. "Don't you think you'll be happy here?"

"I don't know," she told him frankly. "I might be better off somewhere else."

"Let's give it a good try," he begged her earnestly.

"I will," she said with a wan smile. "I know you've spent a lot fixing the house over."

"I'd hoped you'd approve," he said.

"I do. It's just that it was here that you lived with her," she said, knowing that he would not fully appreciate her feelings and not intending to try and make them clear to him.

They strolled along the cliffs, discreetly in the opposite direction from the Richard cottage. She was left gasping at how steep the cliffs were at this point, clinging to Stan's arm as she peered over the edge at several places to see the rocky shore and foam-covered waves lashing against it far below.

She gave her husband a worried glance. "It's very dangerous. Shouldn't there be a fence of some kind? Children could easily topple over here or even adults under the right circumstances."

Stan smiled tolerantly. "You can't fence the whole coastline. All the properties along here are privately owned and there are no young children among any of the families. And we've had no problem of other youngsters trespassing."

"Still I'd worry," she said, gazing down at the distant angry water and rocks. "It was along here you think Jean met her death?"

"Yes."

She gave a tiny shudder. "I won't walk the cliffs often. They frighten me."

Stan put an arm around her waist. "You shouldn't be afraid when you're with me."

"Heights have always bothered me," she confessed.

His handsome face was thoughtful. "Strange. Jean didn't mind them at all. And in the end she took her life here."

She shook her head as they strolled back toward their white colonial house. "I don't even like to think about it," she said.

They went inside and she paused to study the grandfather's clock in the front hallway. Comparing its fancy hands with the time shown by her own wristwatch, she saw that the tall, walnut antique was keeping good time.

She turned to Stan, who was about to go on to the living room.

"You fixed it?"

He halted and turned. "What?"

"You fixed it. The clock, I mean."

He looked at her blankly. "I haven't touched it," he said.

"You didn't?"

"No."

She glanced at the tall old clock again. "Last night when we were here at the bottom of the stairs embracing, it struck seven. I know, because I counted the times it chimed."

Stan looked uneasy. "I didn't notice."

"You had to," she said in a reproving tone. "I spoke of it and your excuse was that the clock wasn't regulated right. It was around midnight when it chimed seven."

Her handsome young husband seemed to have no answer

for this. He stood in silence for a moment and then he said, "Maybe I did adjust it this morning and forgot about it."

"Surely you'd remember?"

"I did a lot of little chores around while I was waiting for you to come down," he said in a tone of slight irritation. "Maybe I changed the clock as well. In fact, now I'm almost sure that I did."

"I see," she said. The unpleasant part of it was that she was certain that he was lying. It was in his face and in his manner. Lying to put her at ease. He was upset by the way the clock had behaved and yet he didn't want her to know it.

She said no more about it at that moment. They went on into the living room and she found her attention engaged by some fine silverware displayed there. Yet oddly enough even their attraction brought back a moment of unhappy memories for her. She recalled that it was a silver candlestick which Stan had used to kill Jean in that fever dream. Now she was staring at a pair of almost identical candlesticks here on the mantel above the stone fireplace.

She said, "Those candlesticks look like the ones I saw on the table by the stairway in your parents' living room."

Stan nodded with a thoughtful look on his handsome face. "You're right. I'm surprised you'd notice them."

Beth blushed with confusion. "Then they are the same?"

"Yes. I've always admired them and Mother offered them to me as a gift when I was redecorating this place. I couldn't refuse."

She was staring at them and thinking that in her fevered nightmare she'd imagined Stan using one of the candlesticks to bash in Jean's head. Even though she knew it had not really happened, she would always vividly recall the dream. And now by a strange quirk of fate the candlesticks would be here before her all the time!

She didn't dare tell Stan what she was thinking. Helen must have kept her secret well. She could not have told any of the others the strange story of her nightmare after her collapse. Beth didn't feel she could ever tell Stan the truth — that she had wakened from that fever bout fully certain that he was a murderer.

Stan was staring at her in an odd fashion. "Don't you like them?"

"Yes," she managed in a small voice. "I do."

His eyes fixed on her in a strange way, he reached up and took one of the candlesticks from the mantel and held it in front of him just as she remembered his doing once before in his parents' house.

He said, "You have no idea how heavy this is." And he weighed it carefully in his hands with that strange light still showing in his eyes.

She stared at him without immediately replying. She was thinking that he seemed obsessed with the heavy candlestick, just as he had before. And it seemed very odd to her that he should have brought them to his own home. If she wasn't so positive that the violent drama she'd witnessed the night of the storm had all been in her sick mind, she would have thought that her husband was a murderer unable to separate himself from the murder weapon he'd used.

Chapter Six

Stan was studying her with an amused smile. "What's the matter?" he asked. "You look frightened."

"Do I?" she said, embarrassed. "I can't think why."

His almost hypnotic black eyes were fixed on her. "You know you have a very expressive face," he said. "It mirrors what you're thinking."

"Not all the time," she protested. "Don't tell me that. You make me feel naked."

He returned the candlestick to its place on the end of the mantel. "I said that as a compliment," he told her. "Not to make you uneasy."

She managed a smile. "In that case I'll feel pleased."

He was looking at her again. "That's one of the differences between you and Jean. I never could tell what was on her mind by her expression. Her face was a mask."

"Really?"

"Sorry," he said, suddenly smiling and bending to kiss her briefly on the lips. "You don't want me talking about Jean. I should know better."

She said, "I don't mind if you feel you must."

He moved on to an easy chair and sank deeply into it. He reached for a newspaper on a nearby table and gave her a knowing glance. "There's no reason why I should," he said.

"Good," she told him. "I'm about to reveal another facet of my character by preparing you a truly appetizing lunch."

"Excellent," he said. "I hope you're a gourmet cook. I'll

wind up fat and contented."

"Don't dream," she warned him. "It's going to be a salad." And she left him to go to the kitchen and prepare it.

She went to the large kitchen with its many white cabinets and began getting ready for luncheon. She planned to make a cold salmon salad with potato and proper garnishings. She also wanted to prepare a custard dessert she thought her husband might enjoy.

There was salmon in the freezer compartment of the large white refrigerator and she began by taking it out and broiling it. While this was going on she busied herself with the other preparations for the meal. Like any new bride she was anxious to impress her husband with her culinary ability.

Taken up by this thoroughly domestic chore, she forgot most of the doubts and suspicions that had been inadvertently forming in her mind. She knew she must subdue them or they could sour her marriage. She was being very silly in allowing a fantasy which had come about as the result of her fever to darken her mind about Stan.

For a while she worked steadily and made definite progress. Then while she was waiting for the salmon to properly chill, she discovered quite a large collection of cookbooks in one of the cabinets. She saw that they were hastily thrown in on the shelf rather than carefully arranged, and so she began taking them out and noting each one.

It appeared that either Jean or Stan had been interested in cooking, and to her knowledge Stan had no special talents in this direction. There were books on French, German, Italian and Jewish cooking as well as several of the large standard cookbooks. One of these seemed to have been used more than the others and slips of paper had been inserted in the book at various places. Opening to one of these, she found it was a recipe written down in a rather cramped, somewhat childish hand. As she flipped through the large cookbook she came on other paper slips with other recipes. And then she discovered a larger piece of paper which showed a drawing of a crab, the Cancer astrological sign done very neatly and typed underneath. Born July 16th, 1947, at 11:34 P.M. This was followed by a typed description of the personality of the individual born at this moment according to the stars. It was both flattering and candid.

Beth noted the words sultry and torrid, which she felt had to be descriptive of Jean. Toward the end of the brief typed horoscope was a short sentence in a warning vein. She read: "Your stars indicate a threat of violence in the not too distant future. Perhaps in two or three months. Take note. H.R."

She stared at the sentence and the initials following it with the feeling that she was intruding on the dead Jean's secrets. A chill went through her and it was increased as she noted the words of warning had been underlined in ink and underneath the typed matter in the same cramped, childish hand which had written the recipes was written: "Stan?"

The damning piece of paper lay exposed there in the book to thoroughly shatter her. The dead Jean had written Stan's name with a question mark after the warning as if to indicate that she felt Stan might be the one to threaten her. She knew that she had given him reason or she wouldn't have put his name down in this fashion.

Had she done it because of a guilty conscience? Or had she noted her husband's name as a hint of anyone who read the brief horoscope; a clue in case anything should happen to her. Beth continued to stare at the accusing slip of paper. Stan had been so thorough in removing all traces of Jean from the house. At least he thought he had. And yet he had missed this rather alarming notation of the dead young woman.

She had an impulse to take the sheet of paper with the

horoscope and hide it away somewhere. Then she decided against this. Better to leave it where it was. It didn't have to mean anything. If she took it and kept it for herself she would be giving it undue weight. So she closed the cookbook with the horoscope still in it and placed it on the cabinet shelf with the other cookbooks. When she had them all arranged neatly, she went back to the luncheon preparations.

But she was haunted by the memory of what she'd read. She saw that her hand was trembling as she lifted a plate from a shelf to the counter top. And once again she had to discipline herself sternly. She knew she must try to forget that horoscope and Jean's notation after it. Either that or face Stan with it and she knew that would solve nothing.

It was evident that Harvey Richards had prepared the reading and given it to Jean. And it was just as evident she had been beginning to worry about what direction her husband's well-founded jealousy would take. Beth busied herself with getting the dessert ready and tried to blot everything else from her thoughts.

She managed to do this surprisingly well. And when she sat down to luncheon with Stan in the pleasant dining room with its view of the ocean, she'd managed some degree of control over her fears and doubts.

Stan complimented her on the salad. "Perfect," he said, over his partially emptied plate.

She smiled. "I'm glad you approve."

"I wish I could be home every day for luncheon," he said. "But unfortunately the business means I have to be in Boston. You can concentrate on dinners and I'll be looking forward to them on my drive home along the crowded highways."

She agreed to give all her kitchen talents to making his dinners memorable. It wasn't until they were having their iced

110

tea following the meal that she had a sudden realization which struck her with such impact she was unable to keep silent about it.

She said, "It's just occurred to me. You said that Jean was born in July under the sign of Cancer."

He looked surprised. "What about it?"

"That's the seventh month, isn't it?"

"Yes."

Her eyes met his. "And last night when that grandfather clock chimed unexpectedly, it chimed seven!"

"So you say," he admitted grudgingly.

"I know it!"

"You make it sound like a great coincidence."

"Well, isn't it?" she challenged him.

"No," he said, tersely. "I don't know what kind of nonsense you have in mind, but I don't go along with it."

"I'm sorry," she said. "It just came to me."

Stan looked at her reproachfully. "I don't favor that kind of thinking," he said.

"I know," she replied awkwardly, "let's just forget all about it."

No more was said at the table. During the afternoon they sat outside for a time enjoying the sun. And later they spent a good hour or two placing wedding presents and personal items in various parts of the house. The big debate came about a large framed photo of her. She'd had it done by a prominent Boston photographer and it was in color with a very attractive frame.

Stan staked out a spot on the living room wall mid-way along it. "This is the logical place for it," he insisted.

She held back. "I think it's too prominent for a personal photograph. I'd rather have a painting there and put my photo somewhere less conspicuous."

Her handsome husband smiled at her. "You are the new mistress of the house. I say your portrait should be given a featured place. This is where it should go."

She pleaded some more but finally gave in to him. Because the photo was a good size and the frame large and heavy, Stan found some special hangers with which to put it up. When it was done he surveyed his work with satisfaction.

"It looks fine there," he told her.

"I'd rather it was a painting or even a photo of you," she said.

"You're too sensitive about such things," Stan told her.

Later in the day she saw Harvey Richard drive away from the cottage with the black-haired girl in the dark glasses at his side. She guessed they must be going out to dinner somewhere. She wondered who this new girl friend of the amorous artist might be, but she said nothing to Stan about it. He always bristled at the mention of Harvey Richard's name. It was better to say nothing about him.

Evening came and they went for a short drive. They planned to go to bed fairly early as Stan would be rising around six-thirty to have breakfast and be at the office around eight. He preferred this so he could avoid the morning rush, and it left him free to leave again at four in the afternoon before the heavy return traffic began.

They took a stroll in the garden before turning in for the night. Stan was especially attentive and she once again put all her apprehensions to the back of her mind. Yet with the darkness she again experienced an eerie feeling about the house and grounds — the sensation that they were being spied on by a third party.

From the garden they could see the lighted windows of Harvey Richard's cottage. The shades were drawn but now and then the shadow of someone showed against them as they went by the window.

Staring at the lighted windows, she said, "He still is entertaining someone."

"That girl is likely there for the weekend," her husband said in a grim tone.

"He has the right to guests," she pointed out.

"Probably someone's wife," Stan said sourly.

"You shouldn't be so ready to criticize," she told him. "If you're going to continue living here as his neighbor, you ought to get rid of some of your tensions."

"I won't allow him to drive me away!"

"I suppose he feels exactly the same," she said.

Stan scowled. "Then it will be a stalemate," he told her. "Let's go inside."

Once again Beth had the same difficulty getting to sleep. Stan fell asleep almost the moment he closed his eyes. But this was not true with her. She lay there staring into the shadows with all kinds of troubling thoughts crowding into her mind. She had expected these first days and nights in the white colonial house to be memorably pleasant and in some ways they had been just that. But there were the other moments!

She even began thinking about Africa and those last days spent at her father's side in an effort to halt the suspicions growing in her mind concerning Stan. She recalled the weakening bout of that mysterious fever which had left her so shattered for some time. And she also remembered the wizened, black face of the old housekeeper warning her that there was a voodoo curse on both her and her father.

Had there truly been a curse invoked on them? Did it explain the mysterious fall which had brought about her father's death? And had it been responsible for the fever which had racked her and given her tormented dreams about Stan being a murderer? Was she even now being tortured by the evil curse so that she was knowing little pleasure in her new home and her marriage?

Or was there something even more sinister responsible for the way she felt? Was there the taint of murder hanging over the house and grounds? Did Stan have something torturing him which he'd kept secret from her? Every so often he came near to offering her a revelation about the past and then seemed to hastily change his mind. He surely hated Harvey Richard. Was it merely because Richard had stolen the affections of his wife, or was it because he believed the amorous neighbor might have murdered the sultry Jean?

Again the old house seemed to creak and groan in a truly alarming fashion. There was a slight wind and somewhere a loose shutter that rattled as if it were at the fancy of a skeleton hand. She tossed in bed fitfully and wished that sleep might come to her.

Then it happened! From below she heard a loud crash. It came clearly above the other sounds and was definite enough to cause her to sit up in bed with a frightened expression on her lovely face.

"Stan!" she cried plaintively.

He responded by tuning to her in the bed and asking sleepily, "What is it?"

"I heard something!"

He raised himself on an elbow. "You what?"

"I heard something downstairs. A crash! As if there might be an intruder down there!"

Stan was sitting up fully awake now. "Are you sure?"

"Of course!"

"You weren't half asleep and imagined it?"

"No," she replied, frightened and annoyed. "I hadn't even gotten to sleep yet."

He glanced at the lighted dial of their bedside alarm clock. "It's after two."

"I can't help it. I haven't slept. And I did hear a loud crash down there. As if someone fell over something."

Stan gave her a resigned glance. "You want me to go down and check?"

"I'd rest better if you did."

He yawned. "That means I have to go."

"I'll go with you," she volunteered.

"No need," he said as he swung out of the bed.

"I will," she said. "It could be anyone down there. Some robber or escaped criminal." And she also got out of bed and groped in the darkness for her slippers.

"You have too vivid an imagination," he said. "I don't know how you managed in Africa."

"Africa didn't frighten me as much as this place does," she said following him out of the room.

In the hallway he turned on the lights and listened. "All I can hear is the wind."

"I heard something else," she said, fear still on her face.

He sighed. "We'll see." And he started down the stairs.

She followed with her tension mounting as they descended into the darkness of the hallway. He turned on the light when he got there and tested the front door to find it locked. He then went into the dining room and the kitchen and tried the back door. It was also intact.

He gave her a resigned glance. "I think you've spoiled my sleep for nothing."

"But I did hear a loud crash!" she insisted.

"If there's nothing in the living room I'm giving up the search," her husband warned her. "It might have been something outside that got caught in the breeze and made the noise."

115

"It sounded in the house!"

They went down the hall and he turned on the living room lights and then stood motionless with a shocked look on his face. He was staring at the shattered remains of her photo which had crashed down to the floor.

A chill went through her. "My photo!" she exclaimed.

He still stood there. "Yes," he said in a tight voice.

She glanced at the wall and saw that the picture hangers he'd carefully fixed in place had been torn away. And in that instant she had a vision of a vengeful phantom form crossing the living room to her photo and tearing it down! She stared at the broken glass on the floor and saw that the ornate frame had bent oddly at one corner.

She gasped, "You put it up there so securely!"

He gave her an uneasy look. "Walls can be tricky. I've had this happen before. I'm sorry."

"You put up two supports and they're both torn out of the wall!"

His handsome face was pale. "That's because that whole section of plaster gave away." He went over and examined the wall and then picked up the photo. He carefully shook off the remaining bits of broken glass from the frame and came back to her with it. "The photo itself isn't harmed. Thank goodness."

She stared at it. In a tense voice, she said, "The frame is broken."

"Not badly," he said. "I can put it back in shape. And I'll measure for the glass in the morning and order a sheet when I get to Boston. I'll bring it back with me when I come home."

She shook her head. "It doesn't matter. I don't think I want it hung again anyway."

Stan looked at her angrily. "Now you're being silly!"

"I didn't want it there in the first place!"

"What has that to do with it?"

"I had a feeling about it," she said.

"What sort of feeling?"

"That it wasn't wanted there," she said tremulously. "That she didn't want it there!"

"She?"

"Jean!"

Stan looked alarmed and dropping the photo onto a nearby chair he hurried to her and took her in his arms. "What kind of madness is this? What has a dead woman to do with your picture falling?"

"Perhaps everything."

He stared at her in silence for a second. "Beth!" he said at last in a plaintive voice. "Beth, don't go on with this crazy ghost talk!"

"It's what I think," she confessed.

"Then you think wrong," he said firmly. "When I put those hangers in I drove them too far and chipped the plaster. I saw the lifted ring of plaster around one of them and knew it would be weak, but I felt the other one was all right. Apparently the plaster around it was cracked too and I didn't notice. It's as simple as that, yet you have to see a ghostly hand in it!"

"You're telling me all this so I won't be frightened," she said.

"I'm telling you the truth and as a sensible person I expect you to believe me," he said.

She bent her head. "I don't know what to think."

"Beth!" he said in a tender, appealing voice. And he put his hand under her chin and raised her face up to his. "My poor Beth. I shouldn't have brought you here. I'll have to consider getting rid of this place and finding another."

"Will you?" There were tears in her eyes.

"I promise," he said.

"I don't think this place is lucky for us."

"Apparently you're right."

"And you have all those hate feelings for that Harvey Richard. And he is our neighbor."

"I know," Stan said wearily, his arms still around her. "I promise that I'll begin looking for another place at once. I want to continue living in Marblehead, so finding what I want isn't going to be that easy. It may take a little time."

"Just as long as I know you are looking!"

"I will be," he said earnestly. "And in the meantime I don't want you to let your nerves get the better of you. No more of that ghost talk."

"I'll try not to think about it," she said.

"I'll expect that," he told her. "I know I made a mistake in planning for us to live here but you mustn't give way to silly panic."

"The fear is very real to me," she said earnestly.

"Only because you allow it to be," he said. "Now we'll go upstairs and forget all about this and try and get some decent sleep for the balance of the night." He drew her to him and kissed her and then he turned out the lights and they went upstairs again.

Of course sleep came no easier to her than it had before. She lay awake until it was near dawn and then fell into a sleep of sheer exhaustion. And once again she was tormented by the old dreams of being lost in the forest and then of seeing Stan murder that blonde-haired girl. Her series of nightmares ended with her racing in fear through rain and darkness to come to the edge of the cliffs. In her desperate flight she was unable to halt herself and so with a scream plunged over the cliff and down to the dark, angry water below.

The scream brought her awake and sitting up in bed. She

saw that Stan had gone and the sun was shining in around the window drapes. Guiltily she got out of bed and went downstairs to discover that he'd made himself coffee and was already on his way to Boston. There was a note on the kitchen table.

"Didn't want to wake you! Have a good day. Will bring the glass back with me. Love, Stan."

She read the note a second time and stuffed it in the pocket of her dressing gown. She felt that she'd somehow failed Stan with her attack of nerves the previous night and then not being up to have breakfast with him.

Going into the living room she saw he'd moved the photo and frame to a table where he'd evidently been measuring for the proper glass size. She moved across the wall and noted that the hangers had come out because of chipped plaster as he'd told her.

With a troubled sigh she went back upstairs to shower and dress for the day in blue and white striped cotton slacks and a white ribbed pullover. She had a leisurely breakfast and went out to the garden to stroll for a little. Then she decided it was time to clean up the mess in the living room caused by the fall of her photo. The broken glass and plaster was still on the floor and rug.

Having prepared herself with dustpan, broom and vacuum cleaner, she went into the living room and began to work. She'd barely knelt before the mixture of glass and plaster when the doorbell rang. With a tiny groan of annoyance she got up and went out and answered the front door.

It was Helen. Her sister-in-law was standing on the front steps dressed in blue denim pants and a red turtleneck shirt. She said, "I thought it was time I paid you a call."

"Come in," she said. "I was just settling down to some housework."

119

"Good for you!" the dark-haired sister of Stan congratulated her. "I won't keep you long."

"I'm glad to see you. With Stan in the city it can be a long day."

Helen was taking in the place. "He surely did make a change here. I like the new decorating."

"Yes. It is pleasant and suits the house."

Helen's eyes caught the mess on the floor. "What happened there?"

Embarrassed, she said, "That's what I was about to look after when you rang. Stan hung a framed photo of me there and in the night it crashed down and broke pretty badly."

There was a strange look on Helen's attractive face. She said, "It surely did break with a vengeance."

"Yes."

"Odd," Helen said.

"The hangers gave way," she said lamely.

"Did they?" Helen arched an eyebrow. "I'd have expected Stan to be more careful. He usually is. What I was thinking is that's the exact spot where he used to have a portrait in oil of Jean hanging. The one done by Harvey Richard."

It shouldn't have come as a shock to Beth but it did. In a very real way it was a confirmation of what she'd been thinking; that there was a ghostly hand behind the incident. She had an idea Helen might be thinking the same thing.

She said, "Yes. I've heard about that portrait."

"You've never seen it?"

"No. Stan removed everything pertaining to Jean before I came here. At least he thought he had. I'm not entirely sure he was all that successful."

Helen gave her a rather frightened look. "You're thinking of ghosts?"

"I suppose it's only natural I should."

"Yes," Helen said. "I understand."

"I've asked Stan to find us another house and put this one up for sale," she said.

"Did he agree?"

"Yes."

"I'm glad," Stan's sister said. "Sometimes he can be stubborn about such things."

"He realizes I'm bothered badly by this place," she said. "And then there's the problem of Harvey Richard still living next door."

"I hadn't thought of that," the other girl admitted.

"All in all it seems wise we should go somewhere else," Beth said.

Helen sighed. "I've wondered why Stan doesn't think about living in some other city rather than Marblehead. But then he is very devoted to Father and Mother and doesn't want to live far from them."

"I don't mind living here as long as we find another house," she said. "Would you like some coffee?"

"I would," Helen said frankly. "But I don't want to be a nuisance."

"You won't be," she told her. "I can do with some myself."

She made a pot of coffee and they sat in the eating area of the kitchen and chatted. Helen, who was a chain smoker, puffed nervously on one cigarette after another.

Beth said, "You smoke too much."

"I know," the dark girl said with a grimace. "But I'm so nervous. Smoking seems to help."

"What makes you so nervous?"

Helen gave her a direct look. Her pleasant young face went in shadow. She said, "Ted's drinking, for one thing. I had no idea it would be so bad."

"Is there nothing you can do?"

"He's very touchy about it," Helen said. "He just tells me I knew about his drinking when I married him and of course it's true."

"But you hoped he'd get over it?"

"I was sure he would. My parents warned me against the marriage. So now I'll just have to try and make it work. I'm sorry he was so mean to you at the engagement party."

She smiled wryly. "Apparently he liked Jean and resented my taking her place."

"He did like her. He's also friendly with Harvey Richard, although Richard is a lot older. Bad pennies!"

"I've seen Harvey Richard at a distance. He had some girl here for the weekend."

Helen stashed out her half-smoked cigarette. "That's a usual practice with him."

"I wonder what Jean saw in him?"

"He can be charming."

"And from all accounts she wasn't particular."

"Just as my Ted is an alcoholic, so she was unfaithful. She was the type of woman who should never have married."

Beth said, "Yet women like her almost always do marry for security. But they mostly pick a man whom they can dominate. Her mistake was in marrying someone like Stan."

Helen nodded solemnly. "If she hadn't finally taken her own life, I'm certain he would have eventually murdered her."

Beth had it on the tip of her tongue to ask the other girl if she was so absolutely sure that Jean hadn't been murdered. But at the last moment she decided to merely say, "I envisioned such a murder in that fever dream I had the night of my collapse in your parents' house."

"I know," Helen said. "You really thought it had happened. Did you ever tell Stan?"

"No. I wasn't sure how he'd feel about it."

"You are probably right," Helen agreed. "I've never mentioned it to anyone. And I don't think you should either. Not even to Stan."

"It left me with a strange, confused feeling," she admitted. "Almost as if I'd really seen it happen."

"You should try to forget about it," Helen said somewhat awkwardly.

"Yes, I know," she agreed.

"Drop by and visit Mother when you can," Helen said. "She's very lonely. And she is so pleased about you and Stan being married."

Beth smiled. "I'm fond of her. I will."

Helen glanced at her watch. "I'll have to go. There's a meeting at the yacht club I've promised to attend. You and Stan must show up there at some of the parties."

"Is he a member?"

Helen was on her feet. "He was a member of one of the clubs when Jean was alive. I imagine he's kept up his membership."

She saw the dark girl out and then returned to cleaning up the mess where the photo had fallen. Now she firmly believed that the phantom hand of the dead Jean had jealously torn the photo down. It seemed so obvious. But she knew she could not talk about it with Stan. All she could do was press him until he found them another place.

The house was strangely silent, she felt. And when her work was done she turned on the television set and watched it for a short while. But she soon tired of it. The postman came and there were several personal letters for her which she read. Then she decided to stroll out in the garden again.

She felt less tense outside. The garden was lovely with several fine beds of flowers and gravel walks between them, with the entire area surrounded by a waist-high green hedge. It was a very clear day and she could see far out across the ocean and note the large number of pleasure craft in the waters off Marblehead.

She was taking in this colorful scene when she turned to gaze in the direction of the Richard cottage, and to her utter amazement saw him walking across the lawn between the two properties and heading for the garden where she was standing. She didn't know whether to hurry on into the house or stand her ground. After a moment's consideration she felt it would be more dignified to remain where she was.

As he came nearer she had a better look at him. He was a big man, perhaps six feet tall and very broad shouldered. He was wearing light fawn trousers and a white sweater over a dark shirt open at the neck. He had the heavy, rather puffy features and paunch of a middle-aged man who both ate and drank well. He was good-looking in a weary way with eyes that were heavy-lidded and thick sensual lips. His hair, which was brown and curly and parted on the side, showed no hint of gray.

He stepped inside the hedge through the opening near the house and offered her a friendly smile. He said, "I'm Harvey Richard, your neighbor. I have brought you a letter left at my place in error by the postman. It's for your husband and I felt I should get it over to you at once."

So his coming over had been motivated by a wish to do them a friendly act. She took the letter from him and said politely, "Thank you. It's very good of you."

He stood there watching her with those disconcertingly knowing eyes. He said, "Glad to do it. Gave me an opportunity to introduce myself."

At least he was honest. She said, "I've seen you driving by."

Harvey Richard nodded. "Yes. I was home this weekend. I would have paid a call to welcome you but I know your husband doesn't approve of me."

"Oh?" She knew her cheeks had gone crimson and she clutched the letter without knowing what to add to the simple exclamation.

The worldly Richard smiled thinly. "I imagine he has told you about my friendship with his first wife."

"Yes, he has," she said quietly.

"I'm not ashamed that I liked Jean and she was fond of me," the big man in the fawn slacks and white sweater said. "But I do deplore the way she died and the mystery surrounding her death."

Beth was sure that Harvey Richard must have some kind of hypnotic quality about him. Ordinarily she would have turned away at his first mention of Jean and gone into the house. But she seemed frozen where she stood, caught by those searching eyes under the heavy lids, the warm rumbling of his deep voice, and the way he had of insinuating that Stan knew more about his first wife's disappearance and death than was healthy.

She said awkwardly, "I wasn't aware that her death presented a mystery. She leaped from the cliffs and her body was found along the shore some time later."

The big man looked solemn now. "I know they claim she took her own life."

"Don't you believe it?"

"Did you know Jean?"

"No. We never met."

"A pity," Harvey Richard said in his soft rumble. "If you had you would feel as I do. That she was a person who would

125

never destroy herself. Especially not in that manner. She was too vain about her lovely face and figure."

She fought to break the spell he seemed to be exerting over her and failed. She asked, "If you believe she didn't take her own life, what do you think happened?"

He gave her a regretful smile. "That is rather complicated. She came to see me that night before she vanished. She said Stan was here and they'd had a bitter quarrel. She planned to leave him and she asked me if I'd marry her."

"What was your answer?"

"I told her I'd be happy to if she would be willing to tie her life to an older man like me. Then she left me to go back and talk to him about the divorce. I never saw her again."

She said, "My husband claims he didn't see her after she went to your place."

"I know," Harvey Richard agreed, those hypnotic eyes seeming to mock her. "That made it rather awkward for me when the police first began asking questions. But I managed to convince them that I had no knowledge of what happened to poor Jean after she left my place."

"Stan thinks you refused to marry her and that is why she threw herself off the cliffs."

"Then Stan is wrong," the big man said softly.

"Or he thinks you could have quarreled and pushed her over," she said.

"I believe he indicated some preposterous story like that to the police," the big man agreed with a hint of ironic amusement. "But when I had finished talking to them, they simply discarded the theory. I am not a violent man, my dear girl, and that is well known in this community. I'm the most unlikely of murderers. I've never been known to lose my temper. Stan, on the other hand, has a reputation for his quick rages. But of course as his wife you must know that!"

She stared at him in disbelief. "Are you saying that Stan may have been responsible for Jean's death?"

"I'm saying that he is temperamentally capable of committing such a crime while I am not. We're very different types, you know."

"I still think she took her own life," Beth maintained.

The big man shrugged. "It's always a possibility. It was a wild night. So stormy! I don't know when we've ever had a storm as bad before or since."

His words swept over her with the shock of cold waves. All at once those lurking suspicions which had been with her since the night of the storm and her collapse came rushing back. Could she have been wrong? Could there have been more to her fevered nightmare than she had been led to believe? Was it possible she'd actually seen Stan murder his wife? But then she remembered the girl had been a visualization of the one on the cover of that mystery novel! Helen had shown her that! So it couldn't have happened!

Still she asked, "Was that the dreadful storm that took place on the night of the Moore's thirtieth wedding anniversary?"

"Yes," he said. "How did you know?"

"I was at their place," she said in a taut voice. "Their house guest."

"Then you know all about Jean's disappearance that night," the big man said. "You were here."

She shook her head. "I became ill that night. And I left soon afterward."

Harvey Richard studied her with new interest. "Now I remember," he said. "You're the girl from Africa."

"Yes."

"Your name came up several times," he said. "And so you and Stan married. That makes quite a romantic story."

"I thought she vanished much later," she said, still wanting to be sure. "Not that night, but much later."

The heavy-lidded eyes mocked her again. "It was that night. Make no mistake about it. I hope I haven't upset you with all this talk, my dear. But I think it's good to get these things out in the open. I think it could be to our mutual advantage for us to be friends."

"What makes you think that?" she asked faintly.

"We are both interested in solving the riddle of Jean's death, for one thing," he said in his assured way. "And it is often good to have a friend near at hand. Someone to call on in time of trouble."

"You see yourself as that someone?"

He bowed graciously. "I will be happy to assume the role. You see, dear Mrs. Moore, I would be dreadfully upset if anything happened to you." He paused to let the words take full effect. "Now I must go. We must be discreet. But my phone is listed in the book and my door will be open to you at any time. Remember that!" And with another bow he turned and walked out of the garden.

She watched his hulking figure as it retreated to his patio and then vanished behind the brick wall. She wasn't sure that any of it had happened. Surely it was all a macabre daydream on her part.

Then she felt the letter he'd brought still in her hands and she knew it hadn't been any daydream but terrifying reality. She turned and fled into the house and threw herself on a divan in the reading room just inside the rear door. She lay there stretched out sobbing.

Chapter Seven

It was time for lunch but she had no desire to eat. She was too filled with horror and fear. She had to talk to someone about that night and the only person she felt she could safely approach at this moment was Helen. Helen had gone to a meeting but she would have to be home soon.

She paced up and down in the reading room, one dreadful suspicion and then another clamoring in her mind. Her head ached miserably and she felt physically ill. She had no car. Stan had spoken of getting her one but there had not been time for that yet. She felt she must get to Helen's place rather than ask her back to see her. She hoped by appearing unexpectedly she would catch the dark girl by surprise and help induce her to tell anything she knew.

Going to the phone, she searched the directory and found a taxi number. Then she put a call through to the taxi company. They promised to send her a cab right away. She washed and fixed her make-up. Then she went to the kitchen cabinet and took the sheet of paper with the typed horoscope and Jean's written comment on it. She folded it carefully and put it in her pocketbook. Then she went to the front door to wait for the taxi.

It came in a few minutes and she got in and gave the driver Helen's address at the other end of the town. As they drove away she caught a glimpse of Harvey Richard standing in front of his cottage. He was pretending to trim a hedge but she could tell he'd gone out there simply to watch her.

The taxi driver was a veteran who took her through the old section of the town with its historic buildings and tourist spots, then by the street with some of the later fine mansions, of which the Moore's place was one, to a modern section where Helen lived with her new husband, Ted Allan.

Helen's place was a pleasant split-level on a dead-end street. Beth hastily paid the taxi driver and got out and hurried up the asphalt driveway to the doorstep of Helen's house. She was relieved to see Helen's car in the driveway before the garage door. She hurried up the steps and rang the doorbell.

After a moment Helen opened the door to her. A look of surprise crossed her pleasant face. She said, "Is anything wrong?"

"I have to talk to you," she said urgently.

"Come in," Helen invited her.

She went inside and mounted the several stairs to the living room with Helen following her. She turned to the dark girl and said, "I thought it best to come here."

Helen showed concern. "I'm glad you did. You look as if a ghost has been chasing you. Let me get you a drink."

"Rye," she said. "Not too strong."

Helen went to the sideboard and fixed one for her and also a drink for herself. The dark girl told her, "Make yourself comfortable."

She sat down in an easy chair but on the edge of it rather than in it. She took a sip of her drink and watched Helen seated on the divan across from her nervously light a cigarette.

Beth looked at her hard. Then she asked, "Why didn't any of you tell me the truth about what happened the night of the storm?"

Helen flinched at the question. "I don't understand."

"Yes, you do," she said evenly.

"You're going way back to the night of your collapse?"

"Yes."

The dark girl puffed on her cigarette and then said, "I don't see what you hope to gain by that."

Beth looked at her directly. "I want to find out the truth."

"Truth about what?"

"Why did you hide the fact that Jean met her death that night? Why did you keep it from me?"

Helen was now thoroughly upset. "I don't know that I did."

"You did and so has everyone else," she said sharply. "I got the impression it was months after that night she vanished and then a long while after that before her body was found. But she met her death that night!"

The girl opposite took a gulp of her drink. "Who told you that?"

"Harvey Richard!"

"Harvey Richard!" Helen said, with an incredulous look on her attractive young face. "Well, it didn't take long for you two to get together."

"That's not important. He told me that Jean met her death the night of the big storm!"

"You know what a liar he is!"

"He wasn't lying about that and you must admit it," she said sternly, keeping up a brave front in spite of her inner fears and sickness.

Helen avoided her eyes. "All right. Jean vanished that night. We didn't know what had happened until they found her body on the shore a couple of months later."

"But you kept it from me that she'd vanished! When you came to the hospital you didn't tell me!"

"No," Helen admitted. "I didn't."

"Why?"

131

The dark-haired girl put her cigarette out and took a drink from the glass she was holding. She took a deep breath and then said, "I was frightened."

Beth stared at her in astonishment. "Afraid of what?" she demanded.

The other girl made a futile gesture. "You came out with that crazy nightmare you had of Stan killing a girl in front of you."

"I'm beginning to wonder if it was so crazy!"

Helen's eyes showed fear. "That's exactly why I didn't dare tell you about Jean vanishing. You were in such a sick, mixed-up state, you would have been sure that Stan had killed her!"

"So you lied to me!"

"I didn't lie, I held back part of the truth!"

"I can't see that the difference is important," Beth told her angrily.

"It wasn't of any importance to you!"

"I don't agree!"

"We kept silent for your good. I discussed it with Mother and she agreed. Then when the telegram came about your father's accident and you had to leave, it seemed even more logical not to say anything about Jean."

"You want to make me believe this was all for my benefit," she said grimly.

"It was!" Helen said, springing to her feet.

"It was to keep me in the dark! To protect Stan!" she said unhappily.

"When you say that you're practically accusing Stan of Jean's murder! Do you realize that?"

She bit her lower lip and nodded sorrowfully. "Yes, I know that," she said in a lower voice.

It was Helen's turn to show anger with her. "Is that how

much your love for him is worth? Do you think he's a killer? Are you willing to take the word of a man like Harvey Richard against that of your husband?"

"No one told me," she lamented. "I was kept in the dark. Why all the secrecy?"

"It was something you didn't need to know!"

Beth jumped up to face her friend. "How can you say that? I was bound to hear of it sooner or later! Surely you should have realized and been frank with me!"

Helen looked away. "There seemed no need. Who else but Harvey Richard would try to fill your mind with suspicion?"

"Even Stan didn't tell me the true facts!"

"He was no more anxious to upset you than any of the rest of us," Helen said.

"Alex," she remembered. "Alex was the only one who was at least partly honest. He warned me against all of you and against the marriage. So he must have known!"

"What is there to know? Stan's wife killed herself. We didn't hide that from you. We simply didn't mention when it happened as you had trouble enough of your own at the time. Later it didn't seem necessary to tell you."

Beth said brokenly, "I believed you when you showed me the mystery novel and I saw the girl on the cover was the same girl I'd watched Stan strike with the candlestick!"

Helen said, "I proved to you that reading the novel had triggered the dream that followed your collapse. You accepted that!"

"And so I didn't question anything else," she said. "But now I know I should have."

"You were too ill that night to be sure of anything," Helen warned her.

"You want me to believe that!"

"It's true!"

"I'll have to take this up with Stan," Beth warned her. "I've never talked to him about it before. But now I have to tell him."

"You shouldn't!" Helen warned her.

"I have no choice!"

"It's not a question of choice, it's a matter of judgment and faith!" Helen told her urgently. "If you let him know that Harvey Richard put you up to this, he'll hate you!"

"No one put me up to anything. I simply found out a truth you all tried to hide from me! And what I want to know now is why it became so important for you to hide it from me?"

"I've already explained," Helen said wearily. "It was for your own good."

"I won't accept that. I entered a marriage I mightn't have if I'd known all the facts," she said. "You've conspired against me and placed Stan in a worse spot than ever!"

"If you'd simply listen to reason," Helen protested.

"You mean more lies!"

"I mean that none of this is of any importance unless you seriously think Stan may have murdered Jean! Do you think that?"

She turned away and closed her eyes. Helen had made a telling point. It did all depend on whether she thought she had married a murderer.

In a near whisper, she said, "I don't know!"

"I thought you loved him," Helen said with reproach in her voice.

"I do."

"Even if he should be a murderer?"

"I don't think he can be," she said, turning to face his sister again. "And yet I don't know why you've all behaved in this way."

"Fear," Helen said. "Simple fear. You ought to know

134

something about it."

"What had you to fear?"

"In the beginning, your story of the murder upset me. At that time Jean was simply missing. So I couldn't prove your account of a murder wrong."

"You could and you did by showing me the picture of that girl on the novel's cover," she said.

Helen shook her head. "That didn't really put your suspicions to rest. It allayed them a little but you're still worried and wondering whether it was a fever nightmare or fact. Otherwise you wouldn't be making such a fuss over this."

"So you kept the truth from me to set my mind at rest?"

"Yes," Helen said. "I thought about telling you when you came back to stay with us. Then you got the message from Africa and went directly from the hospital to your plane."

"You could still have come to the hospital and told me that day before I left. You sent your mother instead."

The dark girl spread her hands. "Maybe I was wrong. Maybe we were all wrong. If I had to do it again I might do it differently. What else can I tell you?"

"I had to find it out from someone like Harvey Richard," she said.

"He told you to cause trouble."

"He didn't know that I was ignorant of the facts," she said. "Whatever else you can accuse him of, you can't blame him for telling me."

"Now what?" Helen asked.

"I'm going to discuss it with Stan."

"It won't be easy for either of you."

"I can't help that. There's no other way."

Helen said, "You could forget it."

"No."

"It would be wise."

"I cannot live a lie," she said. "I must have this out with Stan. If he has nothing to hide, no harm can come from honesty between us."

Helen looked unhappy. "He's going to be angry with me. He will blame me!"

"No. I don't want that. There's no reason for him to blame you. I'm the only one who can take you to task for lying to me. You thought you were helping him."

"I did," the other girl admitted brokenly.

"I'll get a taxi and go back," she said. "I want to be there and ready when he comes."

"I can drive you," Helen said.

"No need."

"Please forgive me," Stan's sister begged.

"Don't ask that so soon."

She was bewildered and filled with all sorts of fears. She felt a need to be alone so that she might try and sort some of her thoughts out before Stan came home and she had to confront him with what she'd learned. He also had carefully avoided telling her the time of Jean's disappearance. He would have a difficult task explaining why.

Harvey Richard had talked to her as if she were in real danger; as if Stan were truly a murderer who might next strike at her. His ominous warning had been shattering on top of the lie he'd so neatly brought to light. Then there had been her own strange feelings about the house and the weird things which had happened since her arrival which had made her believe in Jean's ghost.

She tried to arrange her thoughts and was about to find the phone herself when she heard the front door open. She and Helen both turned to see who it might be. It was Ted Allan who had let himself in, and by his manner and relaxed smile it was plain that the big blonde man had been drinking again.

Helen gave a tiny groan. "This is the last thing we need!"

Ted came slowly up the stairs and joined them. "Well, I didn't know we had a guest," he said drunkenly.

"I'm just leaving," Beth told him.

He blocked her way. "Not on my account. Enjoy the hospitality of our hearth and home! Don't mind me!" And he laughed in drunken fashion.

Helen said, "Ted, please!"

"I know," he told her. "I'm not very popular with your girl friend. Little Beth doesn't like me because I was a friend of Jean's."

Helen said, "Please, Ted!"

He moved over to his wife and drunkenly placed an arm around her. "That's the truth. She doesn't want anything to do with me because I liked little old Jean!"

Beth said, "I don't care who you like. I have to be on my way." And she started for the stairs.

Ted came after her and caught her by the arm. "Don't run away!" he said thickly.

She tried to free herself. "Let me go!"

"Ted!" Helen said, joining them.

Ted seemed to sober somewhat as he said, "Just give me a minute to speak my piece. Okay?"

Beth felt it best to humor him. "All right," she said.

"I have nothing against you," he said.

"Thank you," Beth told him.

"This is a lot of drunken nonsense," Helen said angrily.

"Don't nag me, wife," Ted said in his tipsy way. And then he directed his attention to Beth again. "The thing is I didn't like what happened to Jean. She was a cute number! You know what I mean? She was a truly pretty little thing!"

"I don't see why this concerns me," she said, thinking she couldn't stand much more of his talk.

"Died too young and too bad a death," the big blonde man said, his face suddenly grave. "I tell you she was better looking than you. You believe that?"

"I don't think it important!" Beth declared.

Helen took a step toward her. "I'll drive you home. We can leave now."

Ted moved down the stairs with a drunken man's agility and in this surprise move blocked their way again. "Wait!"

Helen pleaded, "Ted, let us go now and I'll forgive you for the fool you've made of yourself!"

"No," he said with alcoholic gravity. "Want to prove what I've been saying." He glanced at Beth. "Okay?"

"What do you want?" she asked in a tired voice.

"I want to show you Jean's picture. Prove she's the best looking of all of you!"

"No!" It was Helen who cried this out.

Beth stared at her and had a sudden suspicion. She turned to the inebriated Ted and asked him, "Do you have a photo of her handy?"

He nodded. "In the den! Follow me!"

Helen tugged at her arm as she started up the stairs and across the room toward the den. In a taut voice, she said, "Now is our chance to get away!"

"No," she said. "I think I'll look at that photo since he's so anxious for me to see it. I've never seen a likeness of Jean."

Helen showed panic. "He'll never let you go if you follow him in there."

"I think he will," she said. And she left the dark girl to make her way to the library.

She didn't get all the way. Ted came stumbling along to meet her with a mounted photo in his hand. He said, "I told you I had her picture and I'd prove she was the prettiest girl! There!" And he held out the photo for her.

She took it and looked at the smiling likeness of the lovely girl in the photo and knew in that moment why Helen had not wanted her to see it. For it was the same girl whose face had been on the mystery novel cover and whom she'd seen Stan strike with the candlestick!

Ted stood by her swaying just a little with the smell of whiskey strong on his breath. "Well, what do you say?" he asked.

Beth stared at the photo and in a taut voice said, "She is a beauty."

"Knew her when she was a model," Ted went on. "One of the best! Don't know why she married Stan! Stuffed shirt! I'd have married her and she'd have been alive today!"

She handed him back the photo. "Thanks for showing it to me."

Ted seemed to be more sobered as he took the photo. He gave her an uncertain look. "No harm meant. You understand? Just wanted to show you. You're okay!"

"Thank you," she said and she turned and left him standing there with the photo he seemed to treasure looking lonely and rather lost.

She went back into the living room where Helen awaited her with a crestfallen expression on her pretty face. Beth said, "I've seen the photo. Now I know. You played a double trick on me, didn't you?"

"I merely showed you the book," Helen said.

"But you knew I'd jump to the conclusion that the book cover had sent me into a fever hallucination. You didn't tell me that Jean had modeled for the cover of that particular book."

"I knew Stan was innocent. I was trying to protect him. I was afraid you might jump to rash conclusions," Helen said limply. "I'm sorry."

"Now I don't know what to believe," Beth said.

"You still hallucinated," Helen insisted. "I'm certain Stan never followed Jean to my parents' house that night and attacked her. He couldn't have and have disposed of the body before they came back."

"He might have had time," Beth said. "And after her body was in the water long enough, who could tell whether her injuries were the result of a blow on the head or a fall?"

Helen's face was the picture of distress. "Don't talk like that!"

Beth told her, "I'm only letting you realize the things I have to weigh now before I can decide whether Stan is guilty or innocent."

"I'm sorry."

Beth said, "I'm going."

"I'll drive you," Helen told her.

There seemed no point in insisting on a taxi at this moment. She was anxious to get out of the house before the none too sober Ted joined them again. Then it might be difficult if not completely impossible to get away.

She started down the stairs to the front door with Helen at her side. They left the house and got in Helen's car. The dark girl was in a very tense mood while the repeated shocks had had the effect of making Beth coldly accept it all. She was beyond despair!

At the wheel Helen said, "I suppose you hate me for what I did."

"I'm trying not to," Beth said.

"Believe me, I didn't do it to harm you."

"I'd like to think that."

"You must! And it will work out! Jean was a wayward, lovely girl who caused misery to everyone she came in contact with. She left a path of destruction behind her. And her way

140

of life finally destroyed her."

Beth looked out the side window at the passing scenery. "I'm a little late catching up with the facts," she said bitterly.

In a small voice Helen said, "You know now that my husband was in love with her. You heard him admit that."

"He married you."

"After she became unavailable," Helen said unhappily. "I'm sure that since her death he's been drinking more heavily. I know that's what's behind it."

"That doesn't have to be true," Beth protested, feeling sympathy for the other girl despite what she'd done.

"I'm positive it is. So you see I'm also under Jean's cloud as well as you. She touched a lot of lives and tainted them."

"And yet she was such a beauty," Beth marveled.

"A wicked beauty!" Helen said grimly. "She brought my mother unhappiness after her marriage to Stan and did all she could to disgrace our family name. I couldn't begin to list the people she hurt."

"Perhaps Harvey Richard was among them," she suggested.

The girl at the wheel looked disgusted. "If so, I'm sure he was a willing victim."

They drove on through the old town until they reached the white colonial house which Beth would always regard as Jean's house. She let herself out of the car.

Helen leaned across anxiously to speak with her before she could close the door. Her dark-haired sister-in-law said, "Please don't tackle this thing rashly. Stan has also been under a terrible strain. He needs your consideration.""

Beth nodded. "I know all about that."

Helen's look was pleading. "Please go on thinking of me as your friend. And take my advice. Avoid Harvey Richard in the future."

"Thanks," she said. "I'm sorry I had to bring you all the way back here."

"I was glad to come. I'll phone you later," Helen said awkwardly.

Beth shut the car door as the dark-haired girl gave her a final piteous look and then drove off on her way back home to Ted and his maudlin, drunken mood. Beth could not help feeling sorry for her.

She unlocked the front door and let herself in. Glancing at the grandfather clock in the front hall, she saw that it was just four o'clock. At this moment Stan would be leaving his office and going to the garage where he kept his car to begin the drive home to Marblehead.

She went on in to the living room and sank into an easy chair. Her eyes found the spot on the wall where her picture had hung and where Jean's portrait had been displayed before she came to the house. The gaping marks in the plaster were grim reminders of the weird accident that had made her think of phantom hands dragging the photo from its hangings.

Now she knew the whole story, or at least almost all of it. There were important parts which only Start could fill in, if he would speak honestly. Dare he be frank with her if there were blood on his hands? After all the weeks of doubt she was at last faced with a showdown!

Her delving into the past had changed everything. All the values had been transposed. None of the foundations of her beliefs were solid any longer.

What she had to decide now was whether her first conviction that she had watched Stan murder Jean was correct, or whether it had actually been part of a nightmare brought on by her fever. Had she actually seen Stan that night or had the whole fantasy been enacted in her sick mind after she'd collapsed?

When she'd awakened in the hospital she'd been sure she'd seen the murder take place. But Helen had dissuaded her in this belief, chiefly by using the illustration on the mystery novel's cover to shake her faith in what she recalled. But now this hoax had been revealed.

Stan admitted to entering the house and finding her and later calling an ambulance. At some time during the wait for the delayed ambulance to get there through the storm the family had arrived. But had Stan time enough to dispose of the body of the wife he'd murdered between the moment of her collapse and the moment of the family's arrival? That was the important question.

Stan could be a murderer! Harvey Richard's insinuations might be only too correct. And whether Stan had been goaded to the awful act by Jean's evil was not of great importance. Nor was her love for him enough to change the situation. If he was a killer and she'd witnessed the killing, their life together was over. She'd have no choice but to notify the authorities.

With these thoughts coursing through her mind she sat there in the easy chair dejectedly and waited for Stan to arrive.

Chapter Eight

She was still seated there in the living room when she heard the car drive up. She closed her eyes and gripped the arms of her chair as apprehension of the moments to come surged through her. She heard the car door open and close followed by the familiar tread of his footsteps as he approached the rear door.

The door opened and he came in. He called out, "Beth!"

She hesitated for a moment and then in a taut voice said, "Here!"

A moment later he came into the living room. His handsome face wore a smile and he carried a brown paper wrapped piece of picture glass under his arm.

He said, "I have it. I sent one of the girls out to get it at lunch time."

Beth stared at him from her chair. "Good," she said quietly.

Stan placed the glass on the chair with the photo and then turned to her again. Now it seemed he was aware that she was not in her usual mood. His face clouded as he stood before her and asked, "What's wrong?"

She rose slowly from the chair. Giving him a troubled glance she said, "Too many things." And she moved away from him to take a stand by the window staring out at the ocean.

Stan came to her side with concern. He touched her arm. "What has happened? Are you still upset about that picture falling last night? I thought I'd explained that to you."

She turned so that she was looking at him directly. She said, "So many things have been explained for my benefit."

"What exactly does that mean?"

Her eyes met his. "I disobeyed you today."

"Oh?"

"Yes. Harvey Richard brought a letter over that had been wrongly delivered to him by the mailman. So I chatted with him for a few minutes."

Stan looked relieved. "I don't mind," he said. "You needn't be so upset about that."

"Wait," she told him.

He frowned slightly. "What else?"

"In the course of the conversation he told me something."

"What?"

Her look was meaningful. "Something I hadn't been told before. Something everyone has tried very hard to conceal from me."

"Go on," he said.

"I learned from him that Jean vanished and lost her life on the night I had my collapse at your parents' place."

Stan stared at her. "Didn't you always know that?"

"Did you ever tell me?"

"I don't know," he said uneasily.

"I'm sure you do," she argued. "You gave me the impression it had happened much later without actually telling me when it took place."

"I didn't intend to."

"I think you did," she told him. "And Helen put me off the track the same way. It was all a game to confuse me and make me think that Jean either killed herself or was killed later."

He swallowed hard. "Why would anyone want to confuse you about that?"

She gave him a searching look. "Don't you know?"

"Would I ask if I did?" he said in an exasperated tone.

"Helen didn't tell you?"

"Tell me what? What is all this mystery?" he demanded.

"The night of the storm before I collapsed I was certain that I saw you come into your parent's house," she said. "I was standing at the lower landing and first your wife, Jean, came running into the living room as if she were terrified, then you came after her. You looked angry. There were words between you. Next you ran to the table and picked up a candlestick, one of the candlesticks you have here now, and crashed it down on her head. I saw her fall on the carpet with blood spurting from the wound. Then I collapsed!"

A look of horror had crossed Stan's handsome face. "That's sheer fantasy!" he exclaimed. "It's all nonsense! A product of your sick mind at that time. I came in and found you collapsed on the landing and at once called an ambulance. All the rest of the things you've said are products of your fevered imagination."

"That was the night Jean vanished," she said.

"All right! But I didn't kill her with any candlestick!"

"A candlestick would make the same type of wound as a fall," she said. "You could have taken her body in the car to the cliffs and dropped it over afterwards. In the storm no one would have ever seen you."

"I was with you waiting for an ambulance," he said desperately now. "And then the family came. They were there with me when the ambulance arrived."

"Who?"

"All of them! I was the only one who didn't attend that anniversary dinner of theirs!"

"They must have felt you killed Jean or they wouldn't all have banded together in a conspiracy of silence to keep me from discovering she died that night!"

Stan looked crestfallen. "You believe that?"

"How can I help it? Even you kept the truth from me. You told me the facts of her death as you wanted me to know them, carefully concealing the date she vanished."

"You make it seem that I plotted against you!"

"Did you?"

"No," he said. "I love you. I would never do that. I loved you from that first moment I saw you with your father in Africa."

She gazed at him forlornly, wanting to believe him, but still feeling that she had been kept in the dark deliberately and that things were still being concealed from her.

She said, "I love you enough to want to believe that. But I want your honesty now. I want to know what really happened that night. As best as you can tell it."

Stan raised a hand in supplication. "What else can I tell you?"

"The facts you're hiding. There has been too much of that. I had to get the key to all this from our supposed enemy Harvey Richard."

"He is surely not a friend," Stan said grimly.

"What about that night?" she insisted.

"What do you want me to say?"

"I don't want you to say anything but the truth. That seems to have become a rare commodity with your family."

Stan hesitated. "You know how it was between Jean and me."

"It's because I know that I'm terrified for you," she told him.

"There was plenty of cause for murder."

"I'm too well aware of that."

147

He frowned. "I couldn't attend the anniversary party. It was being given by a group of my parents' friends. I talked it over with Mother and she agreed that Jean had smeared our name and her appearance at the party could only cause us gossip and disgrace. I didn't care to attend without her so we both stayed away."

"I know all that."

"I'm giving you the background of that night," he told her. "Passions rose as high as the stormy winds. When I arrived here in this house from work in Boston, the storm was already getting bad."

"I remember it."

"Jean was waiting for me and in a fighting mood. One of the things which irked her was that she couldn't behave as she pleased and still be accepted by the right people here. She wanted to be two people, the wanton adventuress and the respected suburban wife. It wasn't possible."

"So?"

"As soon as I entered she began to take me to task. She blamed me for refusing the invitation to the anniversary party. She wouldn't accept that my mother and father didn't want her introduced to their friends. She blamed it solely on me and my desire for revenge for her having an affair with Richard."

"Did you explain it was your parents' wish that she not attend?"

He let a stubborn expression cross his face. "No. I felt I had no need to do that. It was her behavior which had so embarrassed them. She had a right to suffer for it without any involved explanations."

"I see," she said. "What was her reaction?"

"Bad," he admitted.

"Then you should have let her understand the real reason

for your not wanting to attend the party."

"I didn't," he said. "And the quarrel between us became worse. Recriminations were hurled back and forth. At last I told her what I'd been intending to say for some time. I said I was going to divorce her and had plenty of grounds."

"Did she deny it?"

"Of course. She threatened me and said I'd driven her to seek affection from Harvey Richard by my coldness and neglect of her."

"Was there any truth in that?"

"She must have discovered enough to offer her an excuse," he said bitterly. "Things had gotten bad between us, but again that was her doing."

"So you fought?"

"Yes."

"And then?"

"She went over to Richard's cottage to talk to him and probably to tell him she would be free. I took the car and drove to my parents' place and found you in an unconscious state. I waited until the ambulance came and then returned here."

"Did you see Jean again?"

"Never alive. Not until I viewed her body months later when they discovered it on the shore miles from here."

"That's your story?"

"Yes," he said. "So whether we concealed the night of Jean's death from you or not, it had no importance. We did it simply to protect you. You were very ill."

"I was," she agreed quietly. "And yet somehow the fever made me strangely alert."

He frowned. "In what way?"

"My reactions were heightened. The storm was bad, but to me it will always seem even more overwhelming. All my memories of that night seem to have been sharpened by my condition."

"I find that unlikely," he said. "You probably only think they were sharpened."

Her eyes met his again. "And so my memory of you striking down Jean with that candlestick is equally vivid."

He showed despair. "You shouldn't penalize me for a fantasy you had. A bad dream caused by your illness."

"How are your memories of that night?"

"Chaotic," he admitted. "It was a crisis in my life."

"But you do recall some details?" she persisted.

"A few."

"Can you tell me what Jean was wearing?"

He hesitated. "That night?"

"That night," she said. "Can you?"

He thought a minute. "Yes. I don't know what importance it had. But she was wearing a black gown. I think she'd dressed for the party. Thinking that when she argued with me I might change my mind and take her."

"But you had no intention of that?" she said.

"No. I'd settled it with Mother. I'd definitely made up my mind we wouldn't be going."

Beth heard all this in a kind of fog. Her mind was quickly considering something else. Something which had just come to her and which had great importance at this moment. She had suddenly recalled that in the illustration on the mystery novel cover the lovely Jean had been shown in a vivid red evening gown. Yet in her so-called fantasy she had pictured her in black!

She remembered the entire scene in detail and Jean had been wearing a black evening gown when Stan struck her down. And just now Stan had corroborated that the gown Jean had donned that night was black. She stared at him with frightened eyes.

Conscious of her sudden change, he demanded, "What is it now?"

"You've lied to me!" she said hoarsely.

"Lied?"

"Yes."

"How?"

"The dress!"

"What dress?"

"The black gown you claim Jean was wearing!"

He frowned. "What about it?"

"It proves you're not telling me the truth. Not even after all this!"

Stan showed fear. "Why do you say that?"

"Helen tried to put me off the track by showing me a novel with Jean's likeness on it. At that time I didn't know what Jean looked like. So I assumed it was all a fantasy induced by the novel and its cover. I'd had such strange nightmares before during fever bouts and it seemed a likely explanation."

"So it was! You imagined that killing!"

"I'm not so sure," she told him.

"But I've explained how Jean vanished!"

"Have you?"

"I've given you every last detail of that night," he said in desperation.

She shook her head grimly. "I think not!"

"Why?"

"You've given me the clue yourself. You're still weaving lies for me!"

"You're wrong!" he protested, but he looked uneasy.

"Let me explain," she said. "When I saw Jean on the novel she was wearing a red gown. In my fantasy I saw her in black. If the nightmare had been induced by the book, I'd have seen her in red surely. But I saw her in what she was wearing that

151

night, a black gown. So it couldn't have been any nightmare. I must have really seen her!"

Stan stared at her somewhat dazed. After a moment of tense silence between them, he said, "You don't have any faith in me at all."

"You've shattered it!"

"No," he said bitterly. "Harvey Richard did that."

"I'd have found out from someone else. In some way. Why have you gone on lying to me?"

He shrugged. "Because the truth is too damning."

Softly, she said, "So now we come to it."

He turned away from her. "Why bother to talk anymore? You won't believe me, no matter what I say now."

"I'm still willing to listen," she said.

He turned to her and with a great sigh, said, "All right. You did see Jean that night."

"I knew it."

"But you didn't see me kill her!"

"Go on."

Head down he said wearily, "It began just as I told you with a quarrel here about whether we'd attend the party or not. I told her there was no chance."

"At least that much of what you said was true."

He sighed. "We quarreled. Just the way I told you. She ran into her room and locked the door after her. I sat out here and had a drink and read the papers. I went to the windows to watch the storm and saw that there were lights in Harvey Richard's cottage, so I knew he was home. We'd just sent Rosalie away, so it was almost our first night home alone to-gether and it had turned into a debacle because of the row about the party."

"And?"

"I wandered about the house until I felt it was time the

party would be over. Then I decided to drive to my parents' place and see them for a few minutes. I was about to leave when Jean came out and challenged me."

"About what?"

"She claimed that I was going to the party without her. Going late. I insisted she was wrong and said she could drive over to my parents' place with me if she liked."

"And she did?" Beth said tautly.

"Yes. I realized it was a bad move but it was the only way to satisfy her. We drove slowly through the storm and when we reached my parents' house she told me I'd driven there only to put her off. That I'd meant to go to the party. We had another bitter exchange of words. Then she left the car and hurried into the house ahead of me."

"I saw her come in," Beth said breathlessly. "Go on!"

Stan frowned. "I came after her. Naturally I was angry. My parents hadn't gotten there yet, meaning the party hadn't ended, and she turned to quarrel with me again."

"Yes," she said, tautly, recalling the quarrel and the violence that had followed. "And what then?"

He hesitated. "Then I saw you standing on the landing. You seemed on the point of collapse."

"I was."

"I called out to ask if you were all right. Jean said some hateful thing to me and I brushed past her and went over by the table to reach the landing."

She nodded tensely. "And then you picked up a candlestick from the table and attacked her with it!"

Stan showed bewilderment. "No! Then you collapsed. Before I even reached you, you had fallen."

She stared at him in disbelief. "You're trying to make me think none of the rest of it happened."

"I don't know all that went on in your mind, in your fantasy, but I can tell you that is the way it was. I knelt by you and realized you were unconscious and very ill. I turned to Jean and told her and asked her to come help me with you."

"You did that?" she said dully.

"Yes. I have as clear a recall as you claim for yourself," her husband went on. "I said something angry to Jean again and she made an equally nasty reply and flounced out of the room."

"Then?"

"I knew you were very ill and I decided to call an ambulance. I thought I heard the sound of a car outside and when I went to look I saw it was the lights of my car heading out of the driveway. Jean had decided to go home and had left me stranded."

"She drove home on her own?"

"Yes. I went on to the telephone and put through the call for the ambulance. They said because of the storm they could be a while. Then I went back and knelt by you again."

Beth heard this seemingly authentic account of what had gone on and was almost convinced by it. Much of it fitted in with her own memory of that night. The main variation was what happened after the two entered the room quarreling. She had pictured one version of it in which he'd killed Jean and his story was that at that point Jean had left!

She said, "Then what?"

"The family arrived next. They came in two cars. There was a good deal of confusion and upset when they found that you had collapsed. And still the ambulance had not come."

"Was it long after the family came that it arrived?" She was trying to straighten out the time pattern of his account and see if it seemed logical.

"Maybe twenty minutes later," Stan said. "I saw you safely in the ambulance and my father went to the hospital in

154

the ambulance with you. He made the required arrangements for your care and later Helen drove there and picked him up and brought him back home."

"And you?"

Stan frowned. "I was worried about Jean and what she might be up to. I had Helen drive me here. I found the car in the yard but there was no sign of Jean. There were still lights on in Harvey Richard's place, so I assumed she was over there. After Father returned from the hospital and called to say you were making out all right, I went to bed."

"And?"

"The storm ended during the night. When I got up the next morning Jean still hadn't returned. I then decided to phone Harvey Richard. I did and there was no answer. I went out and saw that his car was gone. At once I decided they had gone away somewhere together."

"You did nothing more about it?"

"No. I felt there had been enough scandal. To make a lot of inquiries would only cause worse talk. I had to go away on business for a few days and so I lost touch with things here."

"And when you returned?"

"Harvey Richard was at home but there was no sign of Jean. Then I became really alarmed. I talked with Richard and he claimed he'd not seen anything of her."

"You believed him?"

"I hadn't much choice. I'm not sure about it even yet. But l knew I could put things off no longer. I phoned the police and had her listed as a missing person."

Beth said, "And in the meanwhile I'd been called back to Africa by my father's accident, I suppose."

"Yes. Mother told me she'd been to see you at the hospital and you'd improved so much you were able to get permission to leave."

Beth gave him a searching look. "Why didn't you give me this version of things at the start?"

"I was afraid you mightn't believe me."

She said, "With all your different stories, I don't know whether to credit what you've said now or not."

His handsome face showed distress. "Whether you believe it or not, what I've told you just now is the truth."

"I keep thinking it could have happened the other way," she said.

"I could never have murdered Jean. That was your imagination. You know you were ill. And you had nightmares of that sort in the past."

"Yes," she said. "That's true. But you and Helen and almost everyone have confused me by keeping the facts from me. Now I'll have to think it out for myself."

"And in the meantime?"

"I'll give you the benefit of the doubt," Beth said. "But I'll be honest and tell you I'm not completely convinced."

He raised a hand in a despairing gesture. "What can I say or do to make you believe me?"

"Nothing at this point," she said. "Let time take care of it."

"Meanwhile you may be thinking me a murderer," he protested.

"I didn't say that."

"You've hinted it."

She said, "I didn't create this situation. You know that."

Stan took her in his arms. "I love you! You must sense that. My marriage to Jean was a dreadful mistake. But I didn't have to murder her to escape from it. I could easily have gotten a divorce."

Beth stared up at his earnest face. "I want to think that. But a momentary rage could have gotten the better of your judgment. That's the thought that frightens me."

His eyes sought hers and there was pleading in them. "I'm not a murderer, Beth."

"I hope not," she said softly.

He drew her close to him and kissed her with great tenderness. She knew that she wanted to believe his story. It was the only way their marriage could survive. And there could no longer be any doubts in her mind that she loved this man. Still, the uncertainty about what had truly happened that stormy night would go on haunting her.

Stan seemed relieved after his supposed confession. After dinner he busied himself with replacing the glass over her photograph and repairing the frame. Then he filled the holes in the wall with mending plaster. It was while he was waiting for the quick-drying plaster to set that she discussed the photo with him.

She told him, "I don't want it hung there again."

He showed surprise. "Why not?"

"It makes me uneasy there," she said. "I'd prefer you'd hang it in a less prominent spot and put one of the other paintings there."

Stan said, "I can't think of any reason for not hanging it back in the same place. It won't fall this time. I'll make sure of that."

Her expression was meaningful as she said, "I don't think you have full control of what happens."

"Meaning what?"

"Helen told me that's where Jean's portrait used to hang. I don't want to compete. Do you understand?"

Stan stared at her. "Are you saying that Jean's ghost caused the photo to fall?"

"It has crossed my mind," she admitted.

He looked upset. "You believe the house is haunted?"

157

"I've heard some strange sounds since coming here."

"That's nonsense!"

"Perhaps so," she said. "But until we find another place I'd just as soon you didn't hang my photo at all. Put something else up there instead."

"You're deliberately being difficult," he accused her.

"No," she said. "I'm trying to avoid any more unpleasant happenings. You are going to try and find a new house for us, aren't you?"

"I am," he promised, though he did not sound too enthusiastic about the idea. "The right sort of houses are not easy to locate in Marblehead."

"Maybe your father knows about some?"

"I doubt it," Stan said. "I can ask him."

When the wall was ready he rummaged in the cellar and found a marine painting which he hung where her photo had been. She took the repaired photo to one of the storage closets and put it away there. She felt that now she wouldn't be deliberately challenging Jean's phantom. She was sure the pleasant white colonial house was haunted.

At Stan's suggestion they drove over to visit with his parents for an hour. She was glad to get away from the house and she also hoped that Stan's father might be able to find them another place. On the drive over she spoke to Stan about a car.

"I need a car for myself," she told him. "You're away in the city every day and it means I'm stranded at the house if I can't get a taxi."

"I'll call my dealer in the morning," Stan promised. "I'll have him send you a small car to test drive. If you like it then you can keep it."

She was pleased at the prospect of being mobile once again. And the thought occurred to her that she might contact some of the local real estate agencies on her own and go out searching for new houses in her car. It would be wonderful not to be tied at home.

Stan's parents seemed glad to see them. They were alone in the big house when Stan and Beth arrived. Stan wandered outside with his father while Beth and her mother-in-law remained in the living room. Once again Beth felt that Andrea Moore was looking less well than she should.

She asked her, "Have you been ill lately? You look very pinched and white."

Staring across at her in the room shadowed with the dusk, the patrician Andrea Moore admitted. "I've not been feeling my best. But I think there's nothing to be alarmed about. The condition will pass."

"You worry too much," Beth warned her.

"Perhaps. How are you managing in your new home?"

Beth gave a resigned sigh. "It's very nice but I'm not entirely happy with it. I've asked Stan to fired something else and sell this one."

Her mother-in-law showed surprise. "You know ocean front houses are not all that easy to come by in Marblehead."

"Then I'll settle for something less."

Andrea's thin, worn face registered mild concern. "You must have some strong reason for feeling as you do. May I ask what it is?"

Beth deliberated a moment before replying. But since they were alone and with the shadowed gloom of the big room to give her a kind of cloak, she felt she might be completely honest with the older woman.

She said, "To be truthful I'm very upset about living in that house. To me it's Jean's house."

Stan's mother stirred slightly on the divan. "I had no idea that would bother you."

"I'm afraid it does," she said. "Some odd things have happened."

"Odd things?"

"Yes."

"What kind of things?" her mother-in-law asked.

"I'd say they were manifestations of an uneasy spirit," was Beth's reply. "Once the grandfather clock chimed at a time when it shouldn't have, then I've heard some very strange sounds as if someone unseen were moving about the house, and my photo came down mysteriously from where Stan hung it."

"And you blame these things on a ghost?"

"To be precise, on Jean's ghost," Beth said, gazing across at the older woman in the near darkness of the room. "I'm bothered by the way she met her death."

"Because she was a suicide?"

"If I were sure she killed herself, I mightn't feel so uneasy," Beth said. "Everything is so cloaked in mystery. It seems to me she may have been murdered."

"Murdered!" Andrea Moore gasped out the word.

"It is possible, you know."

"I've never questioned the police announcement that it was suicide," the older woman said.

"I'm afraid that I have," Beth said quietly.

"Why?"

"I'm not sure about all that happened that night. In fact until a short time ago I didn't know Jean vanished on the night of my collapse when the big storm was under way. You didn't make it plain to me when you visited me at the hospital."

"Didn't I?" Stan's mother asked faintly.

"I'm afraid not," she said. "Neither did Helen nor Stan."

"I'm sure it was just an oversight on all our parts," the

older woman said hastily.

"It's hard to understand how you could all omit telling me the same thing unless it had been by mutual agreement," she said pointedly.

"You're quite wrong. I'm sure as far as I'm concerned, the matter was never discussed," Andrea Moore protested.

"I want to think that," Beth said. "Yet I've still a few things to find out for myself."

"Does Stan know this?" his mother asked.

"Yes."

"How does he feel about it?"

"Not too happy."

"I should think not."

"I've given him an ultimatum about finding us another place," she said. "And he knows it is because I'm afraid to go on living in that house."

"I understand your feelings," Stan's mother said. "But you must also be considerate of my son. He has gone through a great ordeal."

"I know."

The old woman seated across from her in the shadows of the room gave a deep sigh. "You have seen photos of Jean."

"Yes."

"She was truly a beauty."

"I know," Beth said, wondering what this might be leading to.

"Stan fell in love with her beauty without thinking of the character that lovely face and figure might contain. I'm afraid it didn't take him long to find out."

Beth said, "You were opposed to the match, I understand."

"From the start. I could tell what Jean was at our first meeting. She knew that I'd seen through her and she became

161

hostile to me. I tried to warn Stan. But it is hard to reason with a man who has lost his heart to a beauty."

"He told me you'd warned him against her."

"My family has always stood for something in this place," Andrea Moore said with pride. "Perhaps I may be accused of being snobbish and family-proud. If so, the accusation is reasonably just. I do feel very strongly about our good name. And I have expected my children to show that same pride."

"You saw Jean as a threat?"

"That girl had no character at all!" the older woman said bitterly. "She flaunted her looseness before all the town. And her affair with Harvey Richard was an especially bitter pill for me. He also belongs to one of the old families, bohemian that he is in his life style. And it meant that the gossip was being spread among the circles where it hurt me most."

"Did you try to explain this to Jean?"

"I did and I think she kept the affair alive deliberately to humiliate me. I appealed to Stan and at last made him aware of the sort of person she really was. It was then she truly began to actively hate me. She even made me a number of abusive phone calls."

"I didn't know that," Beth confessed.

The older woman gazed at her in the near darkness and in a quiet voice told her, "There are other things you don't know. Among them, the fact that since her death I've been tormented by her ghost!"

Chapter Nine

The older woman's face was shrouded by the dark which had fallen over the room and her figure on the divan was blurred. Beth stared at her in amazement at her weird declaration. It was not anything she'd expected to hear from her mother-in-law.

She said, "You're serious?"

"I'm completely serious," Andrea Moore said. "On more than one night I've looked out my bedroom window to see her ghost staring up at me."

"Why are you so certain what you've seen is Jean's ghost?" Beth wanted to know.

"I recognized her," the older woman told her. "I know it was Jean."

Beth was at a loss to know how to reply to this. She finally came up with, "I didn't know you believed in ghosts."

"I do," the old woman seated beyond her in the darkness said. "I must."

"And why should Jean haunt you?"

There was a pause and her mother-in-law then said, "Jean hated me when she was alive. Now she still stalks me from her grave."

The older woman was so obviously sincere it sent a cold chill down Beth's spine. She said, "I think we should have some light."

"By the entrance leading from the hallway," her mother-in-law said. "You'll find a switch there."

Beth got up and crossed to the entrance and groped on the

wall for the switch. At last her fingers found it and she turned it on. The overhead chandeliers came alive, flooding the big room with a healthy glow.

Feeling more confident in the light, she turned to where the old woman was sitting. Andrea Moore remained at the end of the divan with a resigned look on her lean, pale face.

Taking a step back into the room again, she summoned a thin smile and said, "That's better."

"Forgive me," Stan's mother said. "I ought not to have upset you by mentioning Stan's first wife. When you spoke of having him sell the house, it more or less came into my mind."

"It doesn't matter," she said. But it was true that the reference had upset her. In the darkness the mention of a ghost had seemed especially eerie.

Stan's mother looked at her earnestly. "Perhaps the message I was trying to offer was that you may not escape from the tactics of Jean's ghost merely by leaving that house. I think the ghost can follow you anywhere."

"I feel her influence mostly in the house," she said.

"Are you sure you aren't imagining a lot of it?"

"No," Beth said. "I have heard and seen things. If Jean's restless spirit has managed to return and taunt you, I'm certain I shall also suffer from it."

"I have seen her," Andrea Moore insisted, her thin face pale. "She stared up at me from the lawn below. When I cried out, she vanished. But she returned on other nights."

"Has your husband seen the ghost?"

"No," her mother-in-law said. "I tried to point her out to Stephen, but she vanished each time I did."

"So he is as skeptical about her existence as a phantom as Stan is," she suggested.

"He is," the older woman agreed. "So we must suffer this

164

ordeal on our own. Jean was a very evil person in life and now her evil lives on."

Beth could see the older woman was under a great strain and she felt sorry that she had raised the subject of Jean at all. She told her mother-in-law, "You mustn't allow yourself to become too upset over this."

"I will be all right," Stan's mother said. "I worry about you."

"I'm sure Stan was sincere when he told me he'd find me another house as soon as he could," she said. "And even if there are still some manifestations of Jean's spirit in the new place, I'm certain the atmosphere won't be so charged with her."

"Probably not," her mother-in-law agreed. She rose and came over to Beth and took one of Beth's hands in her bony grip. "Do not mention my seeing the ghost to Stan. It would only upset him and do no good."

The intensity of the older woman's manner was alarming. Beth felt great sympathy for her. "Very well," she said. "If that is how you feel."

"I know I'm right," Stan's mother said. "Stan was tormented by that woman when she was alive. I don't want him to go on suffering through her. So I prefer to bear this alone and in silence."

"I understand," Beth said. "I'll say nothing of what you've told me."

Andrea Moore's weary face brightened a little. "I'm so happy that Stan eventually found someone like you."

The sound of the men's voices as they returned caused them to exchange knowing looks. The older woman moved a few steps away from her toward the living room doorway as Stan and his father came back to join them.

Stephen Moore gave his wife and Beth an interested

glance. "I've been showing Stan where I propose to build the new greenhouse. What have you been discussing?"

"Any number of things," Beth said, managing a small smile. "It must be dark in the garden now."

"It is," Stan agreed. "We'd probably have still been talking out there if the dark hadn't driven us in. I prefer the south corner of the garden for the hothouse and Father thinks it would be best by the wall on the north side."

"I'll likely compromise," his father said. "There's a good spot midway between the two points. Why not locate it there?"

"That sounds reasonable," Stan agreed. "But I'd like to take another look at it during the daylight."

"Come by soon again then," his father said. "Ted Allan has been talking to a local builder and he's agreed to come and put the greenhouse up as soon as he finishes his present job of construction."

Stan's handsome face showed a skeptical expression. "Has Ted actually taken that much interest in the project?"

"He's quite an avid gardener," Stephen Moore said. "He's not at all stupid, if only he'd keep sober."

"Stephen!" his wife reprimanded him.

The gray-haired Stephen Moore showed annoyance on his stern face. "Surely I can speak my mind before Stan and Beth. They are family!"

"I still don't approve of such talk," Andrea Moore said unhappily.

"More of that precious family pride of yours," her husband said with impatience. "I think we'd all be better off for calling a spade a spade. You're trying to dismiss Ted's weakness by keeping silent about it, just as you did Jean's. And you know how badly that worked out!"

"Stephen!" his wife reprimanded him.

Stan's handsome face had taken on a strange look and he asked, "Is it necessary to bring Jean into this? She's been dead for some time. Why not let her rest?"

At once Stephen Moore was contrite. He turned to Stan and said, "I'm sorry, son. That just slipped out. But I must admit it does express my feelings on the matter. We are all aware that Helen has married a drunkard. No amount of silence will change that fact!"

"Nor will undue mention of it help things," Stan's mother protested.

Stephen Moore frowned. "I say, face up to it. And let Ted know how we feel. There's no point in pretending not to notice his lapses into drunkenness. Doing that we're only encouraging him. I say let him know we're aware of it and at the same time give him credit when he deserves it. Perhaps that way he'll one day improve."

Stan had listened to all this with a grim expression. Now, he said, "Father is probably right. Helen made an error in marrying Ted, in my opinion. But now that the mistake has been made, we're not going to help things by ignoring his alcoholic bouts."

Andrea Moore said, "Let us talk about something else, please!"

Stan glanced at his wristwatch. "Time for us to be on our way," he said. He gave his mother a filial kiss in leaving and told his father, "I'll come by early tomorrow evening and take another look at the garden."

"Do that," Stephen Moore said as he accompanied them to the front door.

As Stan drove the car home through the darkness, Beth turned to him at the wheel and said, "Your mother is a very strong-willed woman. I never realized it as much as I did tonight. She seems to take a firmer stand on many things than your father."

Stan nodded. "Father is much more easy-going. Mother has always been family-conscious and that dominates her whole attitude to life. That is why she prefers to sugarcoat the problem of Ted's alcoholism and why when Jean was alive my mother never spoke of her in a critical fashion, though I knew she hated Jean."

"What about when they were together?" she asked.

"That was seldom," Stan said. "And at those times Mother was coldly polite. But Jean got the message and the hatred was mutual."

"Jean's death must have come as both a relief and shock to your mother," she observed.

"The scandal attached to the suicide was hard for Mother to bear," Stan said. "She actually became ill for a few days after Jean's body was discovered. We were all worried about her. But of course she recovered quickly as she has from every kind of blow. Mother has reserves of courage you'd never guess."

"I'm not at all surprised," she said.

Stan's profile was grim as he drove on. "When Jean's cousin came to stay with us for awhile it was Mother who sensed this would mean extra trouble and warned me against Rosalie."

"And it turned out she was right."

"Yes. Rosalie was as bad as Jean, if not worse."

"You've never heard from her since Jean's death?"

"No."

"Don't you think that strange?"

"She didn't keep in close touch before," Stan said. "And it's likely she knows nothing of Jean taking her life. The two had a quarrel and Rosalie left before Jean's suicide. I'd also asked her to leave."

"You think she returned to Boston?"

"Jean appeared to think so. When Jean's body was found, I did my best to locate Rosalie without any luck. She didn't have any family, like Jean. The hotel where she'd lived before she came to stay with us said she'd left without giving any forwarding address."

"That was strange."

"I thought so," her husband agreed. "I even had Alex stop by the hotel and try to get some lead on her but he had no luck. So we weren't able to have her attend Jean's funeral."

They reached the white colonial house and Stan parked the car in the driveway before the garage. As she got out she automatically glanced over in the direction of Harvey Richard's cottage and saw the lights in his windows. It seemed the amorous bachelor was staying at home a lot.

Inside they talked for a while in the living room. Beth found Stan a trifle strained in manner. He moved about the room a good deal in a nervous fashion that wasn't normal to him. He also looked tense. She felt that the continued references to Jean might have bothered him and resolved to try and avoid mention of her in the future if possible.

But she could not give up on asking for another house. As they prepared to go upstairs to bed, she told him, "I mentioned that we'd be finding another house to your mother."

"Oh?"

"She seemed to think it was a good idea."

"I'm sorry you discussed it with her," Stan said a trifle stiffly. "It's early in the game yet."

Beth gave him a concerned look. "But you were serious when you said you'd sell this place and get another?"

"Yes," he said, "but we can't leave here until I do find what I want and that could take some time." There was an evasive quality to his tone which bothered her and made her think that he might not really be going to give her a new home after all.

"It mustn't take too long," she protested. "I can't go on living here indefinitely feeling the way I do."

"I'm keeping that in mind," he said, his sensitive face taking on a gaunt look.

"I mean it, Stan," she said somewhat urgently.

He took her by the arm. "It's very late. Let us go up to bed."

She said nothing more as they mounted the stairs but his attitude worried her. It was hard to say definitely that his decision to look for another house had been altered. But he was surely showing no enthusiasm for the idea.

His goodnight kiss was tender enough yet her fears were not allayed by it. And long after he was asleep she remained awake and worried. Once again she knew troubling doubts about whether Stan had murdered Jean or whether she'd actually taken her own life. She felt that all the family, with the possible exception of his father, had rallied around Stan to try and protect him in the matter of Jean's death.

She also felt there were facts concerning what happened that stormy night of which she was not aware. They were still hiding facts from her. She was positive of it. And while her conscience troubled her for entertaining the thought that her husband might have murdered his first wife, she could not get it out of her mind.

When she finally slept she had another nightmare. This time she was running along the cliffs during a dreadful storm such as had taken place on that eventful night. She was fleeing from something or someone and she was sobbing with fear and breathless. She stumbled on the wet grass and with a cry of terror almost slipped off the cliff. As she lay there gasping a dark figure loomed over her and she looked up into the hate-ridden face of her husband!

"Stan!" she cried out plaintively.

The cry brought her awake and she was aware of being in her own bed and staring up through the shadows she saw that Stan was standing there by her bedside in his pajamas. And even in the near darkness of the room she could read a frightening expression on his handsome face! A menacing expression!

Startled that he should be standing there rather than asleep in bed, she raised herself on an elbow and in a nervous voice repeated his name. "Stan!"

"Yes!" He sounded angry and impatient.

"What are you doing awake?"

He gave her a bitter look. "I woke up. I couldn't get back to sleep. I've just taken a pill."

She eyed him anxiously. "Is anything wrong?"

"No," he said shortly. "Why make so much of it!"

"I'm sorry," she said. "It startled me to come awake and see you standing there looking like that."

"Looking like what?" his tone was curt.

"I don't know," she hesitated. "Upset and angry, I think."

"You think wrong," he said with a withering sarcasm. "There are times when I wonder if your intelligence equals your imagination."

"Stan!" she said in sorrowful reproof.

He at once looked penitent. "I didn't mean that," he said with a weary gesture of his right hand. "My nerves are on edge. I've been pacing trying to get rid of the tension."

"It's all right," she said.

"The pill I took is making me more relaxed," her husband said. "I can get back in bed and sleep now."

She remained on her elbow, raised up in the bed. "I had a nightmare. That's what woke me up."

He settled into bed and in a harsh voice, asked, "Were you dreaming of me murdering someone again?"

"That's not very kind of you!"

"Just curious," he said, not aware how close he'd come to the truth.

She felt that more talk might only lead to another bitter argument. It was the middle of the night and they were both dead tired. So she lay back under the coverings and waited to hear his even breathing. Soon she did and knew that he'd gotten to sleep.

Now she lay awake thinking about how he had looked when she'd suddenly opened her eyes to see him standing there in the shadows above her. Certainly he'd not resembled a loving husband in any way. His expression had been one of hatred. There was no other way to describe it and it had left her badly upset.

Was Stan a stranger to her? Had she married someone who dared not tell her the truth about his past? He had deliberately concealed certain truths from her and later lied to cover up the facts concerning Jean's death. For all that she knew, he had continued to lie to her. And she was beginning to fear him. She would never have believed this possible. But very gradually he seemed to have changed. Was she only now discovering the kind of person he really was?

The next morning at breakfast he showed a different side of his character. He was in good humor, almost jovial, and he was also considerate toward her. He made no reference to the events of the night and instead concentrated on talk about her car.

"I'll stop by the garage on my way to Boston," he told her. "The car should be sent over this morning. This afternoon at the latest."

"There's no hurry," she said.

172

"I want you to have it as soon as possible," Stan told her. "You need to get out and around. Staying alone here in the house could make you morbid."

"And I do need to look after errands and shopping," she said.

Stan was dutiful in kissing her before he drove off toward the town. She returned to the kitchen and the clearing up of the breakfast things feeling much relieved. She was almost ready to forget her doubts and suspicions of the previous night. Stan had seemed a very different person this morning, much more like the considerate young man she'd married.

When she finished with the dishes she hesitated before the kitchen cabinet in which the cook books were stored. She had returned Jean's horoscope with the dead girl's notation of Stan's name on it to the pages of the book where she'd first found it. It had seemed the thing to do at the time. Now she had a sudden impulse to study the horoscope again.

Opening the cabinet she searched out the large cookbook and brought it down. She'd replaced the horoscope about a third way through the book where it had been before. She skipped through the pages and the written notes of recipes in Jean's cramped hand. She frowned slightly not finding the sheet with the horoscope as she'd expected.

Now she went through the cookbook again and much more slowly this time. But she had no better luck. Her pretty face registered bewilderment. The horoscope simply wasn't there. It then struck her that she might have made an error and placed it in one of the other books of the same type and size. So she took down the other books and went through them, but with no results.

She stood there feeling frustrated. She knew she had returned the horoscope to the book. Now it was gone! Someone must have removed it from the book and destroyed it. Stan?

Perhaps. She couldn't be sure. In fact she wondered if she could any longer be sure of anything.

It was about an hour later that the salesman came from the car dealer with a smart little white car which Stan had picked out as a possible selection for her. The young salesman was pleasant and showed her the various points of the car before leaving the keys with her and going back to the garage with another man who had followed him in a second car.

Beth got in the car and started the motor. It seemed to run smoothly enough and she decided to drive a distance down the shore road and back. She did this. And when she'd gone beyond the Richard cottage and mounted a small hill she suddenly saw a familiar figure walking toward her on the opposite side of the road. It was the dark-haired girl with the black glasses she'd seen with Harvey Richard.

The girl also stared at her a moment as she drove by. She had the impression that her sudden appearance in the car had startled the girl. She drove a half-mile further on and then turned and drove back. The girl had vanished from the road. Beth parked her new car in the driveway by the garage and was about to go into the garden when Harvey Richard came around the brick wall of his patio and waved to her.

She nodded and saw that he was coming toward her. She didn't know whether to wait for him or deliberately snub him by going into the house. She decided that she'd speak to him for a moment and then go on her way.

Harvey Richard was smiling as he came up to her. "What a smart little car," he said. "A new purchase?"

She said, "It just came this morning. I'm trying it out. I'll probably keep it."

He scanned the car approvingly with his heavy-lidded eyes. "I know the make," he said. "They're reliable."

"It seems to run well."

174

"Good," he said. He was looking very smart in a fawn suit, white shirt, and brown cravat.

"I went for a drive up the road and I saw the young woman who was with you the other day," she said, watching him carefully for a reaction.

He showed surprise. "You mean Anne?"

"I don't know her name," she said. "But I recognized her. She has striking black hair and she always wears dark sunglasses."

"That sounds like Anne," he agreed. "But then it's a description that would match any number of young women. And as it happens, Anne isn't here today."

She was insistent. "I'm certain I saw her."

"You saw someone who looked like her," he said correcting her with firm politeness.

"I don't know," she faltered. "The resemblance was amazing and she was walking along the road near your place."

"I'm sorry," the big man said in his mocking fashion. "I must insist that it wasn't Anne."

She saw that the argument was getting her nowhere. She said, "I must have been mistaken."

"Evidently."

She said, "I must go in. I have a lot of things to do."

He smiled. "You have a guest, don't you?"

It was her turn to stare at him. She said, "What gave you that idea?"

Harvey Richard said, "I saw you and Stan go off in the car last night just before dusk."

"Yes. We went to visit his parents for a little." She wondered what this had to do with his thinking they had a guest.

"Later, after it was dark," the big man went on, "I strolled out to my patio. I often do at night. And I happened to glance

175

at your place and saw lights in various rooms going on and off as if someone were moving through the house."

She felt a chill of fear shoot through her as in a small voice she repeated, "Someone going through the house?"

"Exactly," he said. "At first I thought it might be some thief and I debated whether I should call the police."

"I don't understand it," she told him. "We left the house in darkness and it was in darkness when we returned, except for the light on the name post which goes on automatically."

Harvey Richard shrugged. "I gave more attention to what was going on over here than I normally would. And I saw the silhouette of a woman's head and shoulders against the curtains. Then I relaxed and knew it wasn't a thief."

"A woman's head and shoulders?" she questioned in a taut voice.

"There could be no doubt of it. She moved on to the kitchen and I saw her shadow again. So I knew you had someone staying there."

She gave him a frightened look. "You are wrong."

"What?"

"I say, you're wrong. We have no one staying with us. No guest. I don't know what you saw last night but the house was empty and in darkness when we returned."

A strange look had come to the playboy's faded face. He said, "I don't like to argue about it. But I don't see how I could have been wrong."

All her thoughts were of Jean's ghost. Had the phantom figure of Stan's first wife taken possession of the house in their absence the previous night? Would that explain the missing horoscope?

She looked at Harvey Richard and said, "I understand you're a great believer in astrology."

"That's true," he agreed.

"Did you draw a sign and type out a reading below it for Jean?"

He frowned slightly. "I think I did. It was quite a long while ago. I'd almost forgotten. Why do you mention it?"

She said, "I found it in a cookbook she'd been using. She'd written some comments on it."

"Really?" the big man in the sports outfit said. "I would like to see it if you have it available."

She sighed. "It's rather strange, but the horoscope has disappeared. I went to look for it this morning and it had vanished."

The heavy-lidded eyes widened a little. "Would your husband have taken it?"

"I don't think he knows anything about it," she said.

"Interesting," Harvey Richard mused. "Most interesting."

"Yes. I've been puzzled by its disappearance."

"Strange things have happened around here since Jean's death," he warned her. "I have ceased to be upset by them. In time you may come to feel the same way."

"I want to leave here," she said grimly. "We're looking for another house."

Harvey Richard showed surprise. "Has Stan really agreed to sell this place?"

"Yes. Why?"

"I didn't think he would. But then you never can tell. I hope you're not planning to move right away. We're just getting to know each other."

"It will likely be some time," she said. "Stan wants to find the right house and not leave Marblehead. There are not that many houses with the things we want available."

"Not with this harbor view," the aging playboy said. "Jean

was very fond of the view from here. I promised to do her a marine painting but I never did get it done."

"Do you do a lot of painting?" she asked.

"Not any more. I've tired of it as I tire of most things," Harvey Richard said. "I'd need new inspiration to get me started again."

"I hope you find it," she said.

"I no longer consider it important," he told her. "And I'd speak to your husband about that woman I saw over here last night. He may be able to explain it. Perhaps his sister has the keys, or even his mother."

"We were with his mother and father," she said. "So it couldn't have been his mother. I can't imagine Helen having keys but I'll ask her."

Harvey Richard nodded. "I'd do that," he said. "Good luck with your car."

"Thank you," she said as she parted from the big man and went on into the house.

She stood in the kitchen staring out the window at the ocean and pondering what Harvey Richard had said. The big man had no reason for making up a story. It had to either be someone to whom Stan had given keys or Jean's phantom figure!

Following the thought that it might have been Jean's ghost, she recalled waking in the night and finding Stan gazing down at her in bed. He'd been standing there in his pajamas seemingly upset. Could the fact that he'd seen the ghost of his first wife have accounted for his strange mood? Was that why he'd behaved so strangely?

She decided to try and reach Helen on the phone. It seemed to her that Helen was the only one who might possibly have a key. She found Helen's number and sat down to make the call.

Helen answered the phone herself and seemed glad to hear from her. "How are you today?" her sister-in-law asked.

"Quite well," she said. She'd made up her mind to show no resentment about Helen's not having told her the full truth at the time of Jean's vanishing. It would do no good at this point.

"Perhaps we can have coffee later in the day," Helen said.

"Maybe. I have a car I'm trying out. I may go downtown shopping. If I do we might meet somewhere."

"Why don't we?" Helen said.

"I called you about something else," she said. "Do you have a key to this house?"

Helen sounded surprised. "Your house?"

"Yes."

"No. Why should I have?"

She hesitated. "I thought Stan might have given keys to you after Jean's death, so that you could keep an eye on the place when he was away."

"He didn't." Helen was emphatic on the point.

"Some odd things have happened," she said. "Certain items have disappeared and I just met Harvey Richard and he told me that when Stan and I were out last night he saw the shadow of a woman moving from one room to another in the house."

There was a tiny gasp from the other end of the line. Then Helen said, "That's creepy!"

"I know it," she said. "I tried to think who might have keys and you seemed the only likely one. Did Jean have any day woman? Any help of any kind who might have been given a house key?"

Helen said, "She did have a woman who came in two days a week. But the woman and her family moved away from here several months before Jean's death."

"In that case any keys she had would have been returned," she said.

"I'm certain of that," Helen said. "Do you suppose Harvey Richard made up that story to frighten you?"

"Why should he?" Beth worriedly asked.

"I can't think of any good reason," the other girl admitted. "You can ask Stan when he gets home."

"I will," she said. But remembering Stan's strange mood of the night before, she wondered if she'd get anywhere.

Helen said, "How about meeting me at the Marblehead Café around three-thirty?"

"That's on the main street, isn't it?" she said.

"Yes. Just down the street from the Tourist Information Office. There's a parking lot by it."

"I know where it is," Beth agreed. "I'll be there."

She put down the phone with a frustrated feeling. She'd been able to settle nothing. Helen surely hadn't been given any key. More and more it began to seem that a ghost was truly involved. She tried to get this morbid thought out of her mind by busying herself with housework.

Shortly after one the phone rang and when she answered it she was surprised to hear her husband's voice at the other end of the line. He told her, "I've called because it looks as if I'll have to remain in the city overnight. The principal from our Chicago affiliate is in town and he wants to work through the late evening and take an early morning plane back home."

Beth was at once uneasy. "Couldn't you drive back late?"

"I'll be tired and after the talks there are a lot of papers to go over. It would be better for me to stay here and get every- thing done. I can pick up a razor and some shaving cream and a clean shirt for the morning. Do you think you can manage?"

"I suppose so," she said. "You know I'm nervous in the house. I don't relish the idea of being here all night alone."

"I'm sorry," he said. "I hate to ask you to do it. You could go stay overnight with Helen or my parents."

"No," she said. "I'll manage. There is one thing bothering me. Does anyone else have keys to this house?"

"Of course not," he said rather irritably. "What gave you that idea?"

"It would take too long to explain on the phone," she said hastily, knowing that mention of Harvey Richard and the ghostly figure would only send him into a rage. She'd have to discuss it with him when he returned.

"What about the car?" he wanted to know.

"I like it," she said. "I think I'll keep it. I'm meeting Helen for a snack at three-thirty."

"Good," he said approvingly. "Keep on the go. It's not healthy for you to remain in that big house alone brooding. I want you to get out and around."

"I will," she promised.

"You're not frightened at the prospect of being alone in the house tonight, are you?" he asked, seeming to be somewhat concerned for her.

"No," she said. "I'll manage nicely." They talked a minute or two more before the conversation ended. She put down the phone with her pretty face in shadow. She'd put on a brave front but she knew a night alone in the house would be an ordeal for her.

Chapter Ten

Beth drove into the town in time to meet Helen as they'd planned. Because of the events of the morning as well as the night before, she was in a tense mood. She was beginning to believe more and more that she had married a murderer. And, even more frightening to Beth, she was beginning to believe Jean's unhappy spirit roamed the grounds and house where she had once lived.

Why was Jean's ghost returning? Was it to attempt an indictment of the one who had sent her to her death? Or was it that after her suicide she'd jealously wanted to go on ruling the life of the man to whom she'd been married?

These were only a few of the questions troubling Beth as she left her car with the parking lot attendant and walked to the small café where she was meeting Helen. The café was almost empty and Helen was sitting at a broad window overlooking the harbor waiting for her. Beth joined her at the table for two and they ordered coffee and cake.

Helen looked somewhat pale. She told Beth, "Ted has been giving me a few problems again."

"I'm sorry," she said.

"He was picked up for driving recklessly and being drunk," she said. "He's going to have to pay a heavy fine and it will be in all the papers. Mother will be furious."

"You can try and keep it from her."

"That won't be easy in these days of radio, television and newspapers. They repeat everything endlessly."

"I know," she agreed.

The waiter brought them their orders and they resumed talking. Helen said, "I've been thinking about that strange story you told me about a woman being in your place while you and Stan were out last night."

"Oh?"

"Yes. And I have a theory as to who it might be."

"Who?"

"Jean's cousin, Rosalie," Helen said.

She frowned. "But as I understood it, Rosalie left before Jean vanished. She hasn't been located since, so it's very unlikely she'd turn up here."

"You never can tell," Helen warned her. "And I have an idea Jean must have given her keys to the house. So your mysterious intruder could well have been that cousin seeing if she could find anything of value."

Beth said, "I'd rather it be her than a ghost, and that seems about the only other possibility."

"I understand what you mean," Helen agreed. "I may be wrong but it came to me."

"I'll speak to Stan about it when he comes home," Beth promised the other girl.

Helen stared at her worriedly over her coffee cup. "Stan may not know. Jean didn't tell him everything by any means."

"I gathered that."

"But you still should ask him."

Beth gave the other girl a worried glance. "Stan isn't coming home tonight."

"He's not?"

"No. He has business that will keep him in Boston."

Helen frowned. "You're planning to remain all night in that house alone? After all you've experienced and heard?"

"Yes."

"I'd say that's foolhardy."

"I haven't much choice."

"Come stay the night with me," Helen said. "Or go to my parents' place."

"I don't want to bother them and you're having a crisis with Ted," Beth said. "I'll stay in my own place."

"I'd go there and stay with you if Ted wasn't in the middle of this drunken driver charge mess!"

"I'll be all right," she promised.

Helen gave her an anxious glance. "If things get bad, phone me. Keep my number handy and call me at any time in the night. I have a phone at my bedside and I'll come right over if you need me. You don't have to feel alone!"

"Thank you," she said gratefully. "Knowing that will help."

"I wish I could do more," her sister-in-law said.

"I'm really not all that nervous," she protested as she finished her coffee.

"It's all this talk about Jean's ghost," Helen said with a sigh. "I think it's people's vivid imaginations, but the stories do make one uneasy."

She gave Helen a significant look. "Your mother claims she has seen Jean's phantom."

Helen looked distressed. "Did she say that?"

"Yes. She didn't want me to tell anyone, but I'm sure the story is safe with you."

"Of course! But Mother saying that, of all people! She is generally so realistic in her attitudes. It doesn't sound like her."

"I was surprised when she told me. She seems to think Jean is returning to avenge herself on the family."

"Because we didn't approve of her?"

"Yes. That's why your mother feels she was singled out especially for the ghostly manifestation. She really was against Stan and Jean's marriage, wasn't she?"

"To the bitter end."

"I think she worries that Jean came to such a violent death. Perhaps there is some question of guilt feelings."

Helen said, "You almost make it sound as if Jean were put upon. That wasn't the case. She caused the gossip and disgrace which turned Mother and the rest of us against her."

"All except Ted and possibly Alex."

Helen smiled ruefully. "My husband imagined he was in love with her, and Alex always likes to take the opposite view on any stand adopted by the family. He enjoys the role of rebel."

"I know."

Helen said, "I don't want to be out too long but I'd like to have a look at your car before I leave."

"It's in the parking lot," she said. "We can go to it now."

They walked down the street and picked up the trim white sedan. Helen was at once impressed with it. She again told Beth to phone her if she became the least bit nervous. It didn't matter what hour. Then they each went their own way. Beth drove slowly back to the white colonial house and decided that the next day she'd begin a search among the real estate dealers on her own. It might save a lot of time.

She parked the car by the garage and walked through the opening in the hedge to the garden. As she was unlocking the rear door she glanced over at Harvey Richard's patio and saw him standing out there with the dark-haired girl in the black sunglasses at his side.

Beth knew that he'd either lied to her about this Anne not being at his place or that she'd arrived after they'd had their conversation. It was hard to say which was the case, but she supposed she should give him the benefit of the doubt. In any event he wouldn't be anxious to have all his affairs made public, so he might have well lied about the girl being there. It made no real difference to her.

She went inside and read for a little while. A fog began settling in from the ocean. And by six o'clock all sign of the sun had vanished and a shroud-like fog had enveloped the house and grounds. She put her book aside and went to the window and stared out. She could barely see the hedge surrounding the garden.

Though she didn't feel hungry she went to the kitchen to prepare something for herself. And while she was working out there the front doorbell rang. Her nerves were so tense she almost dropped the dish she was carrying. She put it down and went to the front of the house and cautiously opened the door. There standing in the gray mist was Stan's brother, Alex. It had been some time since she'd seen the rebellious Alex, and having him arrive at her door without warning was something of a shock.

"Hello," he said.

"You're the last person I expected to see."

The young man with the horn-rimmed glasses eyed her with an amused look. "You're not very hospitable. Aren't you going to invite me in?"

Recovering her poise a little, she said, "Yes. Come in."

He entered the hallway and she saw that he had a gray suit on under his trenchcoat. He took the coat off and said, "I ran into Helen in town. She told me you were going to be alone. I thought you might enjoy company for dinner."

"I would," she said. "Stan is going to be in Boston all night."

"So I understand," Alex said, putting down his coat and following her out to the kitchen. "I'll help you prepare the

186

meal. I do a lot of my own cooking."

She smiled at him over her shoulder. "There's no need."

"I will, just the same," he said. "We're going to have one of those pea-soup thick fogs tonight. It will make driving dangerous."

"Yes. It's lucky that Stan won't be driving home late. I'd do nothing but worry."

Beside her at the kitchen sink he gave her one of his mocking smiles. "I hope you'll worry for me. I have to make the drive back to Boston right after dinner."

"Must you?"

"Yes. I have some things to take care of early in the morning."

"You'll have to drive cautiously."

"I will. It's bound to get better as I reach the Boston area. Here we're more exposed to it." He paused and said, "Hear the foghorn? It's almost directly across from here on Gull Rocks."

She gave a tiny shudder as she heard the droning sound. "It has an eerie tone to it."

"It does a good job," he told her. "You seem unusually nervous tonight."

"I know. I think it's the fog on top of everything else. I can't seem to help it."

They finished getting the dinner ready. Alex took charge of cooking the steaks. At last they sat down to the food in the eating area of the kitchen. Alex had insisted that the meal be kept informal. It was so dark because of the fog she had to turn the hanging overhead light on.

Alex gave her a sharp glance across the table. "Does your steak suit you?"

"It's very good. You're a fine chef," she said with a smile.

"Just an amateur," he said. "This is the first time we've

seen each other for quite awhile."

"Yes."

He smiled mockingly. "I remember the first time I picked you up in Boston to bring you down here to visit my folks. You had all sorts of notions about what a wonderful family we were. I guess maybe you've changed your mind since then."

She said, "I know you all better but I still think you are a remarkable family."

The eyes behind the horn-rimmed glasses were cynical. He said, "Amazing! You still have some illusions!"

"You think so?"

"Yes. You'll remember I warned you against marrying Stan."

She stared at him. "I do. And I've often wondered about that."

"It was an attempt to save you from living here," Alex said. "Do you like this house?"

"No. We're going to find another one."

He chuckled. "Did Stan tell you that?"

"Yes. Why?"

"I wouldn't count on it. Stan has a kind of special love for this place. It will be hard to get him away from it."

"He's given me his promise," she insisted.

"And you still believe him?"

"Don't you think I should?"

"This place has a lot of memories for him," the young man with the horn-rimmed glasses said with meaning.

"You mean because of Jean?"

"Yes."

"I'd think they would be memories he'd want to avoid," she said.

"Don't count on it."

"But they didn't get on at all well. And then there was the

awful business of her death."

Alex gave her a penetrating look. "You only know some of it."

"I realize that. Can you tell me more?" she pressed him.

"Ask Stan about it," he said cryptically.

"He won't tell me anything."

"Perhaps he will at some later time," Alex said. "I still say you'd have been wise to avoid marrying into the Moores."

She attempted a wry smile. "That's not a very nice thing to say."

"It's how I feel."

"You talk in riddles, continually taunting me whenever we meet. Why do you enjoy tormenting me so?"

Alex laughed and sat back in his chair. "I take no pleasure in tormenting you," he protested.

Her eyes fixed on his. "I know that the truth still isn't known about Jean's death. Are you hinting that she wasn't a suicide? That Stan may have killed her?"

The eyes behind the glasses gave no hint of his thoughts. He said, "That's a blunt question."

"I'll accept a blunt answer."

"Did you marry Stan thinking he might be a murderer? If so, that wasn't too smart of you."

"When I married Stan I wasn't aware of the facts concerning Jean's death. As I have discovered them I've become more worried."

Alex said, "But of course you're in love with Stan."

"I think so."

"You don't sound too sure."

"I'm worried."

"That's part of being married," Alex teased her. "There's always something to worry about. It's my main reason for staying a bachelor."

She said, "You're a very strange person."

"What makes you think so?"

"There's so much hate in you," she said seriously. "You are terribly anti-family and you enjoy causing trouble."

Alex looked grimly amused. "You seem to have me all figured out."

"Not completely," she said. "But I know for some reason you dislike everyone else in the family. I've had more advice and sympathy from Ted Allan and Harvey Richard than I have from you."

"Ted the infamous alcoholic and Harvey the aging lothario," Alex said with cold derision. "You pick yourself strange heroes."

"I'm simply stating facts," she said.

Alex looked at his wristwatch. He then got up from the table. "I'm sorry. I have to go. We can resume this interesting discussion some future time."

She rose to see him out. "We invariably seem to end up arguing," she said.

"Argument sharpens the mind," he told her as he put on his trenchcoat.

"In that case it should be good for me," she said bitterly.

Alex smiled at her. "Why so bleak?"

"It's your peculiar charm," she told him. "You always leave me feeling this way."

"I must try to do better next time. Thanks for a good dinner and your lovely company," he said with a trace of mockery in his tone. "Wish me a good passage to Boston."

"Drive carefully," she said as he stepped out into the fog.

"I will," he promised and walked down the steps and soon became a blurred, phantom figure in the mist.

She closed the door after him with a troubled expression on her attractive face. She moved through the shadows of the silent house to the kitchen again. There she could plainly hear the regular droning of the distant fog horn. She was puzzled by Alex's visit.

He claimed he'd come because Helen had told him she was going to be alone. But she had the uneasy feeling that he might have had some other reason. He frightened her a little with his arrogant manner and his sour comments. She sometimes felt he mightn't be as mentally stable as he ought to be.

As she stood there in the glow of the single light amid the gathering darkness, she had another terrifying thought. Could Alex have murdered Jean? Her husband's eccentric brother behaved as if he had some special secret. Perhaps that was the secret he had! Maybe some of the others knew it and it was Alex they were trying to protect rather than Stan. She found this easier to believe than that Stan was a killer.

So Alex had come to her as soon as he'd heard she was alone. And he had behaved in his usual mysterious fashion. Maybe he had been merely sizing her up to learn how afraid she was and thus be able to play on her fears later. It was a most unpleasant thought and she began clearing up the dinner things in an effort to put it out of her mind.

An hour later she had everything taken care of. It was now completely dark and the foghorn was keeping up its mournful wailing. She went into the living room but couldn't settle down to read or even to watch television. Instead she paced up and down, worrying. She once halted to stare at the spot on the wall where it seemed that phantom hands had torn down her photo. She was thoroughly nervous.

After a short time she went to the windows on the side of the house overlooking the Richard cottage and saw the blurred amber glow of his lighted windows barely showing in the fog. If she went over there, would he welcome her and try to calm her? Or would she be an intruder on him and his dark-haired girl friend? She knew that no matter how bothered she was it would take some special desperation to make her cross to the cottage for help.

At last she decided it was time for bed and went upstairs to the room she shared with Stan. It was going to be her first night here alone in this supposedly haunted house! It was a chilling thought and she knew she had to get her mind off such things.

She took her time changing into her night dress and then got into bed before she turned out the remaining light on her bedside table. Now she gazed up into the darkness and heard the distant foghorn. It seemed louder in the quiet of the night. It also had a somewhat hypnotic effect on her. And to her amazement, sleep came to her more quickly than she'd expected.

Of course she dreamed. It was the wildest of nightmares! She went far back to the jungle fantasy in which she was vainly seeking for her mother and never able to find her. This faded and she next found herself running in terror from some unknown pursuer. This time she was fleeing along the edge of the cliffs. And then the dream switched to the living room downstairs and she found herself facing Stan in the middle of the room. But it was a different Stan from the one she had always known; he looked insane and he raised his hands and came slowly toward her as if ready to throttle her! She screamed and backed away!

In that same instant she came awake. She stared into the darkness and realized she was trembling. The house was weirdly silent except for the continual droning warning of the far-off foghorn. She tried to tell herself there was nothing to be frightened of, but she knew that it was no good. She was caught up in a grip of terror!

And then in the far corner of her bedroom she saw something move in the shadows. She raised up in bed and stared at the gradually emerging figure, too terrified to cry out! It took only seconds for the apparition to form into a recognizable likeness of the dead Jean! She stood there solemnly, her long blonde hair falling about her shoulders, her blue eyes staring and her face pale. She was cloaked in some white filmy thing which hinted of the grave!

The ghost remained there motionless and accusing. At last Beth screamed out her fear and this broke the spell. She threw the bedclothes aside and sprang out of the bed and fled toward the door leading to the hall and the stairs. She raced down the stairs and on across the living room until she reached the front door and threw it open.

Then she fled out across the wet grass in the direction of Harvey Richard's cottage. She heard footsteps close behind her and screamed out again as she was struck down by something heavy. She was momentarily stunned by the blow and plunged face downward onto the grass.

At the same time she heard the voice of Harvey Richard calling out to her. She managed to raise herself up a little and respond to his cry weakly. Then she collapsed on the wet grass again as he came running across to her.

She was too weak and confused to be fully aware what was happening. Harvey Richard picked her up in his arms as if she were a child and swiftly carried her back to his place. Her next clear impression was of sitting in an easy chair before a blazing log fire in a comfortable paneled room. A concerned Harvey Richard in dressing gown and pajamas was seated in a chair across from her.

"Are you feeling any better?" he asked worriedly. His hair was rumpled and he looked unlike the debonair man about town he usually was.

"Yes," she murmured. "What happened?" She realized

she was wrapped in a heavy blanket.

The man opposite her said, "I heard you screaming and went to see what was wrong. I found you stretched out on the grass with a spade a short distance from you. You've had a nasty blow on the back of the head and someone must have done it with the spade. But I could see no one."

She was conscious of an aching head with real pain in the back where she'd been hit. She said, "The ghost! I saw the ghost and ran out of the house!"

He was sitting forward in his chair. "What ghost?"

"It was Jean! I saw her clearly!"

He eyed her incredulously. "You're telling me you saw Jean's ghost and it drove you out of the house?"

"Yes."

"Where is Stan?"

"In Boston."

"I had an idea you were alone in the house. That is why I brought you here," the middle-aged man said.

The full terror of it all returned to her. With eyes wide she told him, "I did see the ghost! Just as I've told you!"

Harvey Richards was on his feet, standing gravely before her. The flames leaping in the fireplace played a pattern of light on his jaded face.

In a solemn voice, he said, "I didn't dispute you."

"But you must think me mad!"

"Not necessarily," he told her. "What exactly did you see?"

She clenched her hands and in a taut voice said, "Jean! I saw her! I recognized her!"

"You're sure it wasn't nerves?"

"No," she said piteously. "I saw her pale face and staring eyes. And the golden hair on her shoulders! It looked wet and dripping!"

Harvey Richard nodded. "That's an almost exact description of her."

"It was as if her dead form had emerged from the ocean," she told him.

"Perhaps it was the end of a bad dream," he said.

"No!"

He raised a placating hand. "Let's not worry that point any more," he said. "You left the house unlocked?"

"I raced out and left the door open! The phantom must have been behind me!"

Harvey Richard sighed. "I'd better go over there and at least close the door."

"Please don't leave me alone!" she begged. "It will be all right!"

"I hope so," he said. "Someone did attack you on the lawn with that spade. It could have been a burglar."

"The ghost," she suggested.

"I doubt it," he said dryly.

She looked at him in despair. "You don't believe anything I've told you."

"That's not so either," he said.

"You think I became upset and imagined it all!"

"I'm not sure what was real and what was imagined," he told her. "I realize you've gone through a bad experience. First, I'm going to get you some brandy."

And he did. She sipped the brandy and it made her feel somewhat better. In the meantime he busied himself with examining the bruise she'd suffered on the back of her head.

"Your hair protected you," he said. "It could have been a killing blow if it had been just a little harder and you'd not had that thick hair. As it is you've a nasty bruise but the skin isn't broken."

"It will be all right," she said.

"I probably should try and get a doctor," he worried. "Not that they're easy to get at this time of night."

"Please don't," she begged him. "I'll manage. The brandy is helping."

"Good," he said. "Just try and calm down. Do you mind if I leave you for a moment now? I'd like to check your place."

She said, "If there's someone out there they might attack you."

"I think whoever was there has long since gone," he said. "I'll only be a short distance away and I won't take long."

She considered this nervously. Then she asked, "Is that dark girl in the cottage? I saw you with her on the patio earlier."

He shook his head. "Anne arrived just after I had that chat with you. And then she left after you saw us together on the patio. She has a house in the next town."

"Oh," she said. So it meant she'd be left there alone.

He said, "It will be all right. I'll leave my door open so you can easily call to me if you need me."

She nodded. "If you think you should go over there."

"I do," he said.

He left the paneled room and she heard him go outside. Then she began to tremble again. She speculated on what might happen if he came to any misfortune and she were left at the mercy of whoever had attacked her earlier. She tried to control her fears by taking stock of the room around her for the first time.

It was a study of sorts and along its paneled walls were hung a number of paintings. Many of them seemed to be of the area surrounding the cottage so she assumed they were original works by Harvey Richard. He was a competent artist and the various oils had lots of color.

She knew that Stan would be livid at her making such a

196

fool of herself and coming to the Richard cottage for haven. But she'd not been able to help herself. She had seen the ghost and uncontrollable fear had taken hold of her. She didn't know what had happened on the lawn. Perhaps it was the ghost that had felled her!

It seemed an eternity but it could only have been a few minutes before Harvey Richard returned. The big man came into the room with a solemn look on his jaded face.

She asked him, "Well?"

He said, "I went over and into your place."

"Was everything all right?"

"Nothing seemed disturbed," he said. "When I left I closed the door after me."

"Thank you."

His eyes met hers. "I went up to the bedroom where you saw the ghost and checked."

Fear tensed her again. "What did you find?"

"Not much," he said.

"But you did find something?"

"Yes."

"What?"

He seemed hesitant to tell her. "I don't consider it of any importance."

"Please tell me!" she begged him.

His face showed a strange expression as he said, "I put on the light and over in the corner of the room I found a clump of wet seaweed on the floor."

"Wet seaweed!"

"Yes."

Her eyes widened. "I told you!" she exclaimed. "She looked just as if she'd emerged from the ocean. It was Jean's ghost!"

"I don't know what to think."

"How can you think anything else?"

Harvey Richard acknowledged, "Until I found the sea-weed, I put it all down to your nerves."

"But now you know differently."

He sighed. "The seaweed had to get there some way."

"It was clinging to her!"

"It may have been a macabre practical joke played on you by someone," he said.

"No!"

"How can you be sure it wasn't?" he asked.

"I know."

"That's hardly good enough."

"I'm not the only one who has seen the ghost."

"No?"

"No! Stan's mother has! She told me!"

The big man stared at her. "She told you she saw Jean's ghost!"

"Yes," Beth said. "She saw it several times, so she said."

"A very strange business," Harvey Richard said gravely. "I think we should give it some thought before we discuss it more. Let it rest until morning."

"It must be close to dawn now," she said.

"It's after three," the man in the dressing gown said. "With this fog there'll be no noticeable dawn until late. There's a guest room here and a bed. I suggest you use it."

She shook her head. "Please, I'd rather remain here in this chair."

"It must be fairly uncomfortable," her host worried.

"No. I'm warm and the fireplace is pleasant."

"You really want to remain there in that chair?"

"Yes. If you don't mind," she said. "I'm more apt to rest here than if I go to bed. Is it all right with you?"

Harvey Richard said, "I want you to stay wherever it is

most comfortable for you. If it happens to be that chair, all very well."

"Thank you."

"I'll build the fire a little so it will last," he said. And he knelt to place more logs on it and bank them. When he finished he got up and told her, "I'll go back to my own bed if you don't mind."

"Of course not."

He studied her with concern. "You're sure you don't want a doctor?"

"No," she said. "My head feels better already. If I can get a little rest, I should be all right. The brandy has calmed me a good deal."

"Do you want some more?"

"No. I've had enough," she said.

"My room is just through the door down back," he told her. "Call me if you want anything or you feel nervous."

"I'm sure I'll be all right," she said. "And thank you for everything."

"I'm glad to be of some help," he said. "I only wish I could offer you a satisfactory explanation for what happened."

"Can anyone do that?"

"At this point, I think not," the big man said. "Goodnight."

"Goodnight," she replied.

He left her and she heard him go into his room and close the door. She pulled the blanket close around her and stared into the dancing flames in the big stone fireplace. The new logs were beginning to crackle and the pungent smell of the burning wood filled her nostrils. She found her plight very strange. She had sought haven with the man supposed to be the enemy of her and her husband.

The brandy had made her drowsy. Now her eyes closed

and she fell into an uneasy sleep. She dreamt she was back in Africa again and the ancient housekeeper was standing before her with a look of fear on her wizened, black face as she declared that a voodoo curse had been placed on her and her father!

Chapter Eleven

Beth was suddenly aware that there was someone in the room with her. She opened her eyes and saw that the fire had burned down to a few black and red embers and it was daylight. And standing by her with a robe over one arm was Harvey Richard, fully dressed in a brown tweed suit.

The man with the heavy-lidded eyes said, "I'm sorry to waken you."

"No. It's time I was awake anyway," she said.

"How is your head?"

"It's sore and stiff at the back but I have no headache or other pain," she told him. "I'm sure it will be all right."

His jaded face showed a grim smile. "You are more optimistic than most would be under the circumstances. I give you credit for it."

"I'm so greatly obliged to you."

"Not at all," he said. "Because of my rather Bohemian style of living, it happens that I'm well equipped with dressing gowns and the like. I have one here for you. The bathroom is down the hall. I think you'll find everything you need there. And when you've finished I'll have some hot coffee and scrambled eggs waiting for you."

She said, "I should go straight back to my place."

"Not until you've had breakfast," her host said firmly. "No one will see you go back in this fog. And it is expected to last through most of the day."

She said, "I'm really a terrible nuisance to you."

"On the contrary," he said with a smile. "It happens that I enjoy a pretty female face opposite me at breakfast."

She said ruefully, "I'm sure I'm not very attractive looking this morning."

"But I disagree," he said. "I'll be waiting for you in the dining room when you are ready."

He left the robe on the chair arm and tactfully retired from the study. She let the blanket fall back from her and was upset to find her filmy nightgown was torn in several places and smeared with mud and dried grass. She quickly put on the robe and made her way to the bathroom.

Harvey Richard had not exaggerated when he'd told her there would be almost everything she'd need there. She even found a selection of nightgowns and she replaced her own torn, dirty one with a fresh new gown. She washed and bathed her tender head which was sore to touch. And using a comb and brush which had been provided she managed to get her hair into reasonable shape.

There was even some very neutral type make-up and she used some of the powder and lipstick. By the time she left the bathroom she felt she was at least presentable. She'd also found a pair of slippers among several pairs that were in there.

Harvey Richard rose from his chair at the dining room table and showed delight in her improved appearance. "You look like a different girl," he told her as he pulled out a chair for her.

She sat down. "It would seem you expected an emergency like this to happen any time."

"One never knows," the amorous middle-aged man said with a twinkle in his eyes. "At least my stock of feminine apparel has proved of some practical use." He poured her coffee for her.

She said, "All this is like a kind of nightmare."

The big, sandy-haired man was now filling her plate with scrambled eggs, bacon and home fries of several large chafing dishes on the table. He said, "I understand your feelings."

She said, "I don't know how I'll explain this to my husband."

Harvey Richard said, "Simply tell him what happened."

"He's very skeptical about my talk of ghosts."

"Indeed?"

"I'm sure he'll refuse to believe I saw anything."

Her host said, "It was wrong of him to leave you alone in that house all night. He should have arranged for someone to have stayed there with you."

"He suggested that I go to his sister's or his mother's," she admitted. "But I didn't want to." She realized that in spite of all she'd gone through she was hungry and the food and coffee were very welcome.

"But you decided not to?"

She nodded. "For various reasons."

Harvey Richard said, "Your husband should know you have a level head. It took something out of the ordinary to upset you as badly as you were upset last night."

"I hope he feels that way. I know I did see a ghost."

He gave her a significant look. "You gave an exact description of Jean. And when I went back there I found the seaweed on the floor."

"That's the weirdest touch of all," she said.

"There was something in that room," he said with a sigh. "We know that."

"It followed me when I ran from the house. I'm sure of it," she told him.

Harvey Richard had finished his food and now he sat back with a second cup of coffee. With a solemn expression on his jaded face, he said, "If Jean's ghost is appearing in the house and in other places in the area, there must be some good reason for it."

She gave him all her interest. "Please go on."

He said, "When ghosts return it is usually because they are not at rest. Jean must feel she has unfinished business here and that is why she returns. That follows the soundest thinking in spiritualism."

"What sort of unfinished business?"

"It could be she wants to let us know she didn't take her own life," he suggested.

She said, "That would be a strong reason for her coming back."

"And she may want to point out her murderer or at least harass him until he admits his guilt."

Beth gave her suave neighbor a frightened glance. "You're saying that you think my husband may have murdered her!"

This didn't ruffle him at all. He shrugged and said, "I'm merely pointing out possible reasons for the return of Jean's troubled ghost."

She kept her eyes fixed on him. "You're telling me that you feel my husband is the guilty one. That is it, isn't it?"

"I have the same deep distrust of him as he has of me," Harvey Richard said. "I think he may have killed her in a fit of jealous rage."

"And he claims it might have been you," she said.

"He told that to the police and they considered it a joke," the big man at the end of the table said with a grim smile.

"So?" she said.

"So we must consider why she has not presented herself here to me," he said. "Why I have not been tormented by her restless spirit."

"Because you were innocent in her death?" she suggested.

"It makes sense, doesn't it," he agreed.

"It is Stan and Stan's family she seems to want to settle with," Beth said over her coffee.

"So there you have it," Harvey Richard said. "That has to mean something."

She stared straight ahead, frowning. "There are things about that night of the storm which still elude me. I had a strange illness come over me. Much of what I'm able to recall could be sheer fantasy."

"And then it might be truth," the big man said.

"Yes, there is that slim possibility," she said with her voice low.

"Jean fell in love with me," the big man said. "Stan can't forgive me for that. Nor did he forgive her. There were bitter, violent quarrels. I overheard some of them. They could have climaxed in murder."

She gave him a searching glance. "What about Rosalie?"

"Rosalie?" he said blankly.

"Surely you haven't forgotten her so soon," she said. "I have been told that you and Jean had a few battles because you showed an interest in that cousin of hers."

He looked derisive. "She was only a child. Jean was foolish to be jealous of her."

"Did you give her a reason?" she asked him.

He looked uneasy. "It was Rosalie who provided all the reasons," he said. "She's the same type as Jean was, only younger. I tried to warn her that Jean would be jealous and I think it only made her behave worse."

"The girl did have a romance with you then?"

"A trifling flirtation," he said. "I was truly fond of Jean and I didn't want to ruin that friendship because of this younger girl. In the end Jean sent her away. The trouble was she should have done it earlier."

"Have you seen or heard of her since Jean's death?"

"No. She left here angry at both of us. She said she'd never come back and I guess she meant it."

She said, "So you and Jean made your peace as far as she was concerned."

"Absolutely," Harvey Richard said. "Did your husband say that we hadn't?"

"He hinted it."

"You mustn't listen to him where I'm involved," the big man warned her. "He'll never give you a fair opinion of me."

She smiled wanly. "So it seems. And now I find myself deeply in your debt."

"Not at all."

"I'll try not to cause you any more trouble," she promised.

Harvey Richard said, "I've been glad to be of some small help. I just trust that your husband understands."

"I'll make it clear to him," she said.

The heavy-lidded eyes of the middle-aged man studied her. "I only hope you haven't made a mistake in your marriage," he said.

She looked at him soberly. "I have had that said to me before."

"Really? May I ask by whom?"

"Stan's brother, Alex."

He arched an eyebrow. "A very strange young man. But he apparently has suspicions about your husband's role in Jean's death."

"He doesn't say that outright."

"But it means the same thing."

"Perhaps," she said reluctantly. "I'm not too sure. Alex enjoys talking in riddles. He likes to play a mysterious role."

"Still to suggest you made a mistake in marrying his

brother is a serious statement," the man in the tweed suit warned her.

"He must have some reason," she admitted.

"And it has to do with the death of your husband's first wife," he went on. "Don't try to close your eyes to that. Remember what you saw last night."

Fear shadowed her face. "I don't think I'll ever be able to forget it."

"You should leave that house," the big man warned. "And perhaps you should also leave your husband as well."

She gave him a strange look. "You think so?"

He hastened to raise his hand and say, "Don't think I'm trying to win you for myself. That is not so. I am sufficiently occupied in a romantic way for the moment. I'm simply trying to give you my best advice."

"I thank you for it," she said, rising. "Now I really must return to my own house. If I should be seen leaving here it could cause unpleasant talk against us both."

He rose from the table at the same time as she did. He said, "I'm well aware of gossip's poison. I have endured a good deal of it. But you needn't worry. The fog will give you safe cover."

She went to the door. "Thank you, again," she said. "As soon as I'm dressed I'll return these things you've let me have."

"No hurry," he assured her. "As a matter of fact, I'll be leaving shortly and be gone for most of the day. Just put the things in one of your closets and bring them back to me tomorrow or the next day. Whenever it is convenient for you."

"Very well," she said.

"Do you want me to go over with you?" he offered.

"No," she said. "I have no fear of the place in the daytime. It is at night I become upset."

"Good luck," he said, and he remained standing in the doorway as she hurried across the fog-shrouded wet grass to her own house.

She thought of his impeccable behavior and felt that it was much at odds with the picture her husband had presented of him. And she began to wonder if Stan hadn't exaggerated Harvey Richard's faults in order to hide his own.

Reaching the front door of her own place she went inside. But no sooner had she stepped into the hallway than she had the eerie feeling that she was not alone there. She almost turned and fled back across the lawn again but she fought to control her fears. She didn't want to make a spectacle of herself again.

Forcing a false courage she moved on out to the kitchen. Everything there was just as she'd left it. She was about to turn and go out to the hall and up the stairs when she heard a soft footstep on the stairs. And then another! Someone was coming down! She stood there motionless in her fear!

And then a frail figure presented itself in the doorway of the kitchen. It was Stan's mother! At the sight of the thin woman in the neat black suit and small black hat with an austere expression on her lined face, she thought she might faint. Andrea Moore was the last person she'd expected to find waiting for her so early in the morning.

"Where were you?" Stan's mother demanded anxiously.

"I left here in the night," she faltered. "Something happened."

"Please explain yourself!" the older woman said.

"Stan left me here alone last night."

"I know that," her mother-in-law said impatiently. "That is why I am here. I had Stephen drop me off before he drove to Boston. I thought I'd see how you were making out and you could drive me home."

208

Beth gave her an anguished look. "I panicked in the night! I saw Jean's ghost in my room! I was attacked as I ran across to Harvey Richard's cottage. He came and rescued me and gave me shelter for the night and breakfast."

Her mother-in-law looked horrified. "You spent the night in that man's house?"

"I was lucky that he came to my help. Can't you understand?" she said.

The older woman looked shocked. "You say you saw Jean's ghost and then you were attacked?"

"Yes. Someone struck me down with a spade. Harvey Richard found it beside me when he picked me up."

Andrea Moore gave her a frightened look. "I don't know what to say," she told her. And she made her way to a nearby chair and sank into it.

She told her, "Everything happened just as I've told you."

The older woman's face was ashen. "Do you think that Stan will believe you?"

"He must!"

"He hates and distrusts that Harvey Richard for taking Jean from him. You know that."

"This was different. Harvey Richard was a perfect gentleman. He couldn't have behaved any better."

"And you spent the entire night there?"

"From the time I ran from this house," she said.

"It's too bad," Andrea Moore lamented.

Beth gave her mother-in-law an accusing look. "You know about the ghost. You told me that you've seen it several times."

The old woman shook her head unhappily. "I shouldn't have said anything. I put the fear in you."

"No!"

Her mother-in-law eyed her in a despairing way. "It was

wrong of me to mention it. And it was doubly wrong of Stan to leave you here in this house alone, knowing all that we do."

These words caught Beth's attention. She at once asked, "What do you know? I'm sure it has been kept from me. You all try to hide things from me!"

"Nothing to concern yourself about," the old woman said. "You can ask Stan."

"I do and he doesn't give me any satisfaction."

"Then he must think you know all that you should," the older woman said. "This has upset me completely. Would you mind driving me home as soon as possible?"

"No," she said. "Just give me a few minutes to dress properly." And she hurried upstairs.

The strain of the meeting with Andrea Moore and rushing up the stairs had started her head aching. She changed from the makeshift outfit lent her by Harvey Richard and put on a tweed skirt and sweater. Her mother-in-law's reaction to what had happened was worrisome. She might have known that the family-proud old woman would be bothered only by the possibility of scandal.

She gazed with troubled eyes at the corner of the room where she had seen the phantom figure of Jean. And she pictured the pale ghost in her mind's eye. Even with Stan at home she would find it almost impossible to sleep in this room again. She intended to give him a time limit on their finding somewhere else to live. She would give him a week and no more.

Going back downstairs, she found Andrea Moore huddled in her chair and looking almost ill. She told the older woman, "I can take you home now."

"Thank you," her mother-in-law said getting up.

On the drive to the family mansion Beth told the older

woman, "I'm sure we'll solve all our problems by leaving that house."

"You may be right," Andrea Moore said.

"I'm sure of it," Beth told her from the wheel.

Her mother-in-law gave her a troubled look. "Do you think you should tell Stan about last night?"

"I can't very well not tell him," she said. "I've always tried to be honest with him."

"But he may not understand," her mother-in-law warned her.

"I'll have to risk that," she said. "I've shown faith in him. Now he'll have to show some in me."

"I hope that he does," Andrea Moore said in a weak voice.

It was still so foggy that she had to drive with her lights on. She dropped her mother-in-law off at her home and then because she didn't want to go directly back to her own place she drove to the car agency and told them she intended to keep the white sedan. It took a short time to look after the papers involved and then she was free again.

Still reluctant to return to the white house on the cliffs, she headed for Helen's place. She was fortunate to find Stan's sister at home. But Helen was fully occupied with her own troubles.

"Ted's gone off on another drinking spree," she lamented. "And this trouble with the police for drunken driving still not settled."

"Can't you reason with him at all?" she asked as they sat in a small room off the main hallway.

Helen shook her head. "No, I don't know where it's going to end."

Beth said, "I'm sorry for you. And for Ted. But I've also got my own problems."

"I'm sorry," Helen said. "You got through the night all right?"

"I didn't," she said bluntly. And she went on to tell the whole story including the arrival of her mother-in-law and her reaction.

Helen listened sympathetically. "You mustn't mind Mother," she said. "You know how strict and old-fashioned she can be. She thinks only in terms of the family's good name."

"I had no alternative but spend the night at Harvey Richard's cottage," she said.

"Stan may be difficult about that," Helen warned her.

"He couldn't expect me to stay in that house after what I saw," she protested.

"I doubt if he'll believe in your ghost."

"Why not? His mother has seen the phantom. And I have an idea he's seen her himself."

Helen stared at her. "Why do you say that?"

"I woke up the other night and he was on his feet, standing there in the darkness with a strange expression on his face. I thought it was anger, but now I think it was fear. I couldn't understand it then but I think I do now. He likely saw her as well."

"I hope so," Helen said. "In that case he'll be more willing to accept your story."

"He had better," she said. "And I'm giving him notice that I want to leave that house in a week's time at the most. I don't care what he finds or where it is located. Anything will do to get away from there."

Helen looked at her with troubled eyes. "You must have had a truly, dreadful experience."

"I couldn't go through it again," she said solemnly.

Helen said, "Why don't you stay here until Stan gets

home. I can do with the company and it will keep you from being alone in that house."

"I'll stay for awhile," she said. "But I want to get home before he arrives."

"Isn't he supposed to be coming early today?"

"Yes. But the fog will slow him down if it doesn't get any better."

"I hadn't thought of that," Helen admitted.

She sighed. "It was a strange evening last night. I even had Alex for dinner you know. I wonder how he made out getting back to Boston."

Helen said, "He did go to your place then. I let him know you were alone."

"So he said."

Helen looked troubled. "Maybe I shouldn't have told him."

"Why do you say that?"

"I don't know," Helen said. "He talks and acts so strangely a lot of the time. He worries me."

"He was all right, beyond his usual arrogant attitude," she said. "I was glad to have him through the dinner hour. It became dark so early last night."

"Yes," Helen said. But she spoke in an aloof manner as if she were thinking of something else.

Beth said, "Why does Alex seem to hate all the rest of you so?"

Helen smiled bitterly. "He's very unhappy himself and so he wants to see the rest of us in the same predicament. He doesn't care what he says."

"So I've noticed," she agreed.

Beth remained with her troubled young sister-in-law about an hour longer and then drove back to the white colonial house. The fog appeared to be lifting and the place did not seem quite so gloomy.

When she got out of the car she glanced in the direction of the cottage and saw that Harvey Richard's car was gone, which meant that he'd left as he'd promised. She hoped that Stan would soon get home as she felt really isolated with her nearest neighbor gone.

She hadn't long to wait. She'd barely parked her own car and gone inside when Stan drove up. He came into the house to greet her with a smile on his face.

"Where have you been?" he asked.

"Helen's," she said. "I just came back. You must have left Boston at noon."

"I only worked the half day," he said. "And the fog cleared so I had a good drive back." He took her in his arms and kissed her. "Sorry about last night. How did it go?"

"Lots of time to talk about that," she said evasively. "Don't you want something to eat first?"

"You're right," he said. "I didn't stop in Boston for any lunch."

"I'll get one ready for us," she promised.

She kept busy in the kitchen trying to think of how she'd tell him her story. She was almost certain he was going to be upset and wanted to present it to him in the best possible way. When she had the lunch ready she called him and they had it in the eating area of the kitchen. The fog had drifted out to sea again and now there was some faint sunshine.

He smiled at her across the table. "We had a busy time last night, but I kept worrying about you being alone down here. I know how you feel about the house."

"It was a strain," she said.

"I think you should have gone to Helen's place."

"Ted is giving her a bad time."

"Again?"

214

"Yes. And he's already going to have to face a drunken driving charge."

Stan looked gloomy. "You'd think that would wise him up some."

"It doesn't seem to have," she said.

Stan frowned. "We tried to persuade Helen not to marry him but she wouldn't listen."

"I think she loves him."

"Then that's unfortunate," her husband said. "I doubt if he is going to change."

"I felt I couldn't stay the night there with her so worried," she said.

He studied her closely. "So you braved it out here."

She took a deep breath. "Yes and no," she said.

He showed surprise. "What do you mean?"

"I tried to be brave about staying here, but it didn't turn out very well," she said. And she then proceeded to tell him exactly what had happened up to her returning to the house and finding his mother waiting for her.

Stan's face had shadowed. When she finished, he said, "I can't believe it!"

"Why not?"

He got to his feet and gave her a look of contempt. "That you would humiliate me so!"

"I didn't want to have any of those things happen," she said plaintively. "They simply happened!"

He said angrily, "You let your nerves play tricks on you and put yourself in Harvey Richard's hands, knowing how I feel about him?"

"He was the closest neighbor. The one I would obviously turn to!"

"There was no need to run in a panic to anyone!" Stan raged.

"How do you know?" she demanded, rising.

"I've seen you let yourself go in a panic before," he told her.

"This was no panic! I saw Jean's ghost! I recognized her!"

"I don't believe it!"

"Then don't!" she said, angry now herself. "I was attacked on the lawn! It's only good luck that I wasn't hurt badly!"

"You're telling me that the ghost assaulted you as well?" he asked derisively.

"If you weren't so anxious to prove me wrong, you might be able to evaluate all this and see what it means," she challenged him.

"I know it meant your placing yourself in Richard's care and that offends me enough," her husband said.

"Harvey Richard treated me as a gentleman should. I have nothing but praise for the way he behaved!"

"Naturally!" Stan raged. "He wanted to use the situation to help clear himself of any responsibility in Jean's death. He can use you as a character witness."

Beth looked at her husband coldly. "You might also need me in that respect!"

"What?" he looked startled.

"I mean you too have been under suspicion. And I can't ever forget what I was positive I saw that night," she said. "Your position in all this isn't so safe."

Stan was plainly shocked. "If you're saying that I killed Jean, you're crazy!"

"Just as I was supposed to be mad with fever that night," she told him. "I think up until now everything has gone your way. But it may change."

She gave him a final reproving look and then turned and left the house. She crossed the garden and the lawn beyond the hedge walking straight to the edge of the cliffs. The fog had vanished now and there was some sunshine. She stood there with an expression of unhappiness on her pretty face as she stared out at the ocean.

The wash of the waves on the rocks below filled her ears so that she could hear nothing else. She remained there lost in her misery. She had feared that Stan's reaction might be less than sympathetic. But faced with the reality of his anger she found it overwhelming.

While she knew that Harvey Richard might be all the things her husband contended, she could not complain about the way in which he'd treated her. He had come to her aid in that eerie moment in the night when the pale ghost of Jean had stalked her. She could not do less than give him credit for this, even though Stan was so angry about it.

She regretted her bitter words against her husband. But Stan had egged her on to saying desperate things. But were those desperate things what she really thought? Had she ever completely absolved him from guilt in Jean's disappearance and death? Perhaps not. The fever dream had etched the scene of murder too strongly in her mind. And even if it had been no more than a nightmare it would always haunt her.

Once again she felt she was being opposed by all the Moore family. They would rally to Stan's defense and she would be the outsider in the wrong. Perhaps Jean had felt this way. It might have driven her on to the wild behavior of which she'd been accused. Being Stan's wife was not all that happy a role.

She felt something touch her elbow and turned with a start. It was Stan who had come to where she was standing and had placed his hand on her elbow. He looked a good deal subdued and there was a contrite expression on his handsome face.

He said, "Forgive my stupidity."

She stared at him. "Are you really asking my pardon?"

"Yes."

"I can hardly believe it," she said.

"I was wrong to rage at you the way I did," he said with a sigh. "I knew that the moment you left the house."

She said, "I wish you had known it before."

"It was a shock to me. Knowing you ran to him for aid and spent the night in his house."

"You left me alone here," she said.

"I admit that. I shouldn't have."

"I should think not," she said. "You knew how nervous I was."

"I expected you to spend the night somewhere else."

"But you really didn't make any preparations for that," she told him. "You let it happen without thinking of me."

"I've apologized," he said. "After all, what difference does it make. You know what Richard is. It's not a case of Jean all over again."

"Hardly," she said.

"I don't know what this ghost was," her husband went on. "We'll have to investigate that. But I'm certain we'll find some explanation for it."

"I can't think what it might be at the moment," she said, wondering about her husband's change of temper and what had really brought it about.

Stan gave her a troubled look. "The main thing is that there be no quarrel between us. What happened in the house must never happen again."

"You began it," she reminded him. And she debated whether he'd made this quick about face to make sure she was on his side. Was he really guilty and trying to protect himself in this way?

"I'm sorry," he said, "I'll be more careful in the future.

And I'll surely not put you in a position where you'll have to turn to Harvey Richard again. I don't want that."

"We must leave here. I'll give you a week to find another place," she said. "If you haven't found anything by then, I'm moving out to a motel."

Stan looked pained. "Be reasonable!" he protested.

"Those are my terms," she said.

He stared at her in concerned silence for a moment. Then he said, "All right. I'll do my best." And he took her in his arms and kissed her.

She accepted his kiss and embrace. Yet she was still numbed inside from the way he'd behaved earlier. She was willing to try and save their marriage but she was beginning to doubt that it would be possible. With so much mutual suspicion and doubt they would find it an uphill struggle.

Stan placed an arm around her and they slowly strolled back to the white colonial house. When they went inside she decided to go upstairs to her room and change into a dress. It was warmer now that the fog had vanished. She mounted the stairs and entered their bedroom. Then she stopped short and let out a despairing cry!

Her exclamation of dismay brought Stan up the stairs on the double. He came to her side and then let out a shocked cry of his own. For their bedroom was a shambles! Someone had torn and upset everything. The dresser top had been emptied and the items strewn wildly on the floor! The closets had been ransacked and the clothes hurled this way and that! Every single thing in the room seemed to have been vandalized!

Chapter Twelve

Beth stared at all her valued belongings now torn and scattered, and in a dull voice said, "I don't believe it!"

"It's mad!" Stan said, his tone echoing hers.

"When I left the house with your mother, everything was all right," she said.

"Was that when you were last up here?"

"Yes."

He looked at the wrecked room grimly. "Then someone got in here and did this between the time you left this morning and now. Likely before I returned here."

"Who?" she said blankly. "Why?"

"I don't know," he said. "Are the other rooms on this floor all right?"

"I'll see," she said. And she quickly left him to make a check. She made an inspection of each of the other rooms and nothing had been touched. The vandalism had been directed only against their bedroom.

Stan was waiting for her in the hall. "Well?"

"All the other rooms are in perfect order," she said.

"Just our bedroom," he said. "What can it mean?"

"Perhaps it's a follow-up to last night," she ventured.

"Last night?"

"The ghost," she said solemnly. "Surely you've heard of a poltergeist, a malicious ghost?"

Stan's eyes narrowed. "You're going to try and tell me a ghost tore up that room."

"Poltergeists have been known to cause such damage. They sometimes do it in front of people. Make chairs fall over and that kind of thing."

"You think the damage in there was done by a poltergeist?"

Her eyes met his. "The vandalism has been confined to that one room."

"So?"

"I saw the ghost of Jean in the corner of the room last night," she said. "I know you don't believe me, but I did."

Stan shook his head. "I don't know what to say."

"Something is surely happening here," she said. "Now you have solid proof of it."

"It still doesn't make me accept the existence of Jean's ghost," he warned her.

"Give me some other explanation," she said.

"Enemies," he said. "Is Harvey Richard at his place today?"

"No," she said. "So you can't blame him. He left before I did this morning."

Stan looked disappointed. "He might still have something to do with it."

"I can't think how," Beth said.

"What now?"

"Clean the mess up," she said. "Maybe as we do we'll come across some clue as to who did it."

"The house was locked," Stan said. "At least it was when I got home."

"It was," she assured him. "The only time it was unlocked was last night when I was at the Richard cottage. But nothing was harmed then."

"There has to be an answer," Stan said, standing there dismally staring into the ransacked room.

She said, "The most constructive thing we can do is clean up the mess."

He nodded. "All right."

They began the major task. And it took all the rest of the afternoon. They halted for dinner and returned to the task in the early evening. They had cardboard cartons in which they placed anything which was beyond salvage. The cartons were soon filled as the malicious spirit which had perpetrated the damage had been quite ruthless.

Several of Beth's loveliest dresses were ripped beyond repair. It was a miserable task, and by the time the room was in order it was dusk.

Stan said, "I'll take these cartons down and leave them by the garbage."

"Yes," she said quietly. She went over to the bedroom window to look out and saw that it was now raining fairly heavily. And there were lights in the Richard cottage. Their neighbor had apparently returned.

Stan made several trips downstairs with the cartons. Then after the last one had been carried down she went below to the living room. She was seated in one of the easy chairs when he came in to join her.

"It's raining," she said.

"Is it?" he asked wearily. "I hadn't noticed." And he sat down heavily on the end of the divan opposite her. Then he groaned. "I should have called the insurance company. I think our policy covers vandalism. Now we've cleaned it all up."

She said, "You have the cartons of destroyed things as evidence of what happened."

"That's right," he said. "I'd better make the call right away."

She remained where she was as he crossed to the desk

phone and put through the call. When he finished he turned to her and said, "They'll send an appraiser in the morning."

"Good," she said.

Stan gave her a meaningful look. "And when he gets here, you'd better concentrate on talk about bad neighborhood kids rather than poltergeists. I don't think insurance companies guarantee against ghost damage."

She gave him a reproving look. "You just won't accept it, will you?"

"That Jean came back and wrecked our room? No!"

"I'm positive she did," Beth said. "I saw her there last night. And I have an idea you may have also seen her ghost at some time and not told me anything about it."

Her husband looked terribly guilty. "What gives you that wild idea?"

"I remember one night I woke up and you were standing by my bed as if you'd just seen something that had frightened you," she said. "Was it Jean's ghost?"

Stan said, "I promised I'd not lose my temper again, but if you keep on this kind of talk I may break the promise."

"You're still refusing to be frank with me, aren't you?" she said.

"Because you ask me questions I can't answer," he protested. "From the time I married you I've had to contend with your nerves. You've never been well since you lived in Africa and had that fever. Why not admit it? You imagine things!"

She offered him a bitter smile. "Is that to be your story? Is that what you'll tell people if anything happens to me?"

He stared at her in shock. "Don't say things like that," he told her in a tense voice.

"You drive me to saying them," she told him. "And remember, I expect to leave this house within a week. I meant that."

"I must have time," he insisted.

"I've told you how much time you have," she said. "You can make your plans accordingly."

"There may not be another house we'd like available!"

"There are always motels."

Stan said, "You expect me to leave my home and move into a motel?"

"Yes."

"And if I refuse?"

"I will, in any case," she said. "What happened up in that room was the last straw."

"It should be reported to the police," he said. "They might find who did it."

"I very much doubt that."

"The insurance people will probably insist that it be reported," he said.

"I don't care about that," she told him. "I've made up my mind and I've warned you."

"All right," he said with a sigh.

But the argument had raised another barrier between them. And it made it clear to her how far they had drifted apart. They said little to each other as the evening wore on. The rain became a downpour although there was no fog as there had been on the previous night.

The grandfather clock in the front hall chimed midnight and this was the signal for them to go upstairs. They mounted the stairway to the second floor in silence. On the upper level the sound of the rainstorm was much more noticeable. They went into the bedroom in a weary silence.

Beth felt a reluctance to sleep in the room as she prepared for bed. But she knew any objections she might raise would be resented by her husband. So she said nothing. But even with the lulling sound of the rain she was not able to get to sleep at once. She lay in bed half-expecting to see that pale ghost appear in the corner of the room at any moment.

Then the phone on their bedside table rang out shrilly in the darkness. Stan reached for it and answered it. Beth listened and became gradually aware that it was an urgent call from Helen and that Stan was upset.

Finally, he said, "All right. I'll come over!" And he returned the phone to the table.

She raised up on an elbow. "What is it?"

"Ted Allan smashed his car up again," her husband said. "This time someone in the other car is badly hurt. They've taken Ted to jail and Helen wants me to go and see what can be done."

"Now?"

"Yes." He was already out of bed and dressing.

She said in an alarmed voice, "What about me?"

"You'll be all right," he said. "I'll only be gone a half-hour or so."

Beth sat up in bed, panic surging through her. "Stan, I don't want to be left in this house alone."

He was putting on his jacket. "You certainly can't come to the jail," he said.

"I could wait in the car," she pleaded.

Stan looked obstinate. "No," he said.

"You're deliberately trying to be cruel!"

"I want to see you behave like a woman, not a silly girl!" he retorted angrily.

"Stan!"

But he was already on his way out of the room. He had turned on the bedside lamp so she was not entirely in darkness. Now she got up and threw on her dressing gown and put on her slippers. She went downstairs but he had left the house and she could hear the sound of his car as he backed out of the driveway.

She was alone!

Alone in the house which terrified her!

She stood there for a moment deliberating what she might do. She moved across to the window and saw that there was still lights in Harvey Richard's windows. The playboy stayed up late. The rain had eased a little but it was still coming down heavily.

She wondered how bad the accident had been and whether Ted Allan had been hurt or not. He couldn't be hurt too badly if they were taking him to jail. She decided that she would go back upstairs and dress and then drive over to Helen's place in her own car. By that time Helen might be in the house. It seemed a good idea.

She crossed the shadowed living room to the foot of the stairs and was about to start up them when she heard what she was sure was a moan. It was the kind of moan that hinted of the grave and ghouls. She hesitated for a few seconds and then the anguished cry came again! This time she knew it had come from their bedroom!

Fear took hold of her and she turned and raced across to the front door and throwing it open ran out into the stormy night. She almost stumbled as she went down the steps and then clutching her dressing gown close to her she took a few steps across the wet lawn. When she was a sufficient distance away she glanced up at the bedroom window and saw the shadowed outline of a woman's head and shoulders against the drawn shade.

This was exactly the way Harvey Richard had described the phantom intruder he'd seen moving from room to room that other time. She gave a cry of fear, certain that she was seeing Jean's ghost. The figure vanished from the window. But Beth knew she could not go back in there and she did not want to go to Harvey Richard's cottage.

The keys for her car were upstairs in the bedroom so she couldn't even seek shelter in the car or drive it away dressed as she was. The only thing she could think of was to put as much distance between herself and the house as she could so she hurried on toward the cliff's edge.

She bent her head against the rain and sobbed out her fear and misery. She was drenched now and trembling from the cold and wet. She reached the path along the cliff's edge and began walking along it.

Down in the darkness below she could hear the angry waves lashing against the rocks. It was here on a similar night that the unhappy Jean had either jumped or been pushed to her death. Beth bit her lower lip and prayed that Stan would soon return. She glanced over her shoulder at her own place with the bedroom window showing light and the lights in the windows of the Richard cottage. The temptation to seek his help again was great.

She halted and made a decision. She would go back along the path and make for the cottage. She was sure Harvey Richard would help her and Stan was to blame for the situation in any case. So she didn't care whether he became angry again or not. Again she lowered her head against the rain.

She'd gone about a third of the way along the twisting, narrow path when suddenly she had a feeling of not being alone. She raised her head and saw directly in front of her, and only a dozen or so feet away the ghostly figure of the dead Jean!

Beth froze with horror as she gazed at the pale, expressionless face and the long flowing blonde hair of the dead girl.

And then as she stood there a third figure emerged from the darkness. This newcomer appeared out of the field and came between Beth and the phantom Jean.

Crouched and with a walking stick in her hand was the dark-clad figure of Andrea Moore. Stan's mother let out a kind of savage snarl and then raised the walking stick and struck the phantom across the face with it.

There was a frantic cry from the phantom figure as she stumbled back on the slippery surface of the cliff's edge and then with arms raised high in an effort to save herself vanished over the side to the darkness far below. It all happened in a matter of seconds!

Next Andrea Moore turned to Beth with the walking stick still raised high. Her thin face was distorted with rage and there was a light of madness in her eyes.

"You must go as well," she hissed.

"No!" Beth cried and came out of the spell which had held her there motionless. She turned and began to race along the cliff's edge pursued by the mad woman.

All at once there was a frantic scream from her pursuer and Beth hesitated and glanced back over her shoulder in time to see Stan's mother vanishing over the bank of the cliff. The older woman had stumbled on the slippery ground and gone over the edge to her certain death on the rocks below!

Beth was now sobbing aloud in a state near hysteria. She advanced to the edge of the cliff and stared down into the darkness. There was only the lash of the waves on the rocks. Slowly she turned away and began stumbling towards the Richard cottage.

But she didn't get that far. She'd no more than reached the point where the phantom had gone over the cliff when she came upon Harvey Richard standing there. He was gazing over the side with a frown on his jaded face. He seemed oblivious to the rain or to her.

Beth advanced to him and in tormented voice cried, "Two of them! The phantom and Andrea Moore over the cliff!"

This caught the big man's attention and he fixed his heavy-lidded eyes on her for a moment. There was coldness and anger in his face. He made no reply to her, but turned and began walking swiftly back to the cottage.

"Please!" she begged him to come back to her.

But he kept walking. She stood there in a kind of mental fog. After a moment she saw the lights of the cottage go out and then heard his car start and the headlights go on. Then he was driving away.

She began to stumble back across the lawn in the direction of the house. She'd just reached it when the lights of an approaching car appeared and she was blinded by the glow of its headlamps. Then the lights went out and Stan emerged from the car to come to her and take her in his arms.

"You shouldn't have come out here," he told her.

She looked up at him and gasped, "Your mother and the phantom over the cliff! Harvey Richard knows!" And she collapsed.

When she came to it was daylight and she was in a white-walled hospital room. Stan was seated by her bedside and at the sight of her opening her eyes he at once took her hand in his.

"I've been waiting for you to come to," he said.

She stared around her. "Where am I?"

"The local hospital," he said. "You were in pretty bad shape between the shock and the drenching you had."

Her eyes met his. "What happened?"

His handsome face wore a pained look. "Don't you remember?"

She considered and then it all came rushing back to her. Too much flowed into her mind. A wild series of ugly happenings which she could scarcely believe.

She said, "Your mother?"

"Dead. We found her body this morning on the rocks."

"Oh, Stan, I'm so sorry," she said.

"I know," he sighed grimly. "We found the other body not too far from her."

"The phantom?"

"No phantom," he said. "It was Rosalie, Jean's cousin. It seems she came back here and played the ghost under Harvey Richard's direction."

"Rosalie!"

Stan said, "She and Jean looked very much alike. And Rosalie was a lot friendlier with Richard than any of us guessed."

"But none of you knew she was back here," Beth said.

"No. It's my opinion she disguised herself in a dark wig and dark glasses and returned to stay with Richard. I didn't guess that it might be Rosalie."

She stared at her husband. "Then Richard was behind it all."

"It begins to look like it," Stan said grimly. "We have some loose ends to take care of. I think when the police look inside Harvey Richard's cottage they will find the wig."

"Where is he?"

"No one knows. He drove off somewhere. The police are now looking for him."

She brushed a hand across her forehead. "I still don't understand a lot of it. Why your mother was involved and all that."

"We'll be able to talk about this more later," Stan promised as a nurse came into the room. "I'm going to leave for a little. Everything will be all right. Don't worry!"

Stan bent to kiss her and then left. The nurse saw that she had something to eat and then gave her two tablets. They apparently had a sedating effect as she at once drifted off to sleep.

She rested through the rest of the day and all that night. It was the following morning before Stan came back to her room again.

Beth was much more herself now and able to sit up in bed. She said, "I want to leave here as soon as possible."

"The doctor says this afternoon," Stan told her.

"It doesn't seem soon enough," she told him.

"The doctor won't let you go until then," he said. "And I'm taking you to Helen's place for a few days."

She at once remembered Ted's accident and asked, "What about Ted?"

"The fellow in the other car wasn't injured badly after all," her husband said. "But I think Ted has finally learned his lesson. He says he's joining AA and there'll be no more drinking."

"Do you think he means it?"

"The judge is taking it into consideration in ruling on his case," Stan said. "So he'd better mean it."

"I hope so for Helen's sake," she said. "I don't want to go to her place. I'll be a nuisance."

"She wants you to come," Stan said.

"What about you?"

"There's a room for me as well," Stan told her.

"Have they caught Harvey Richard?"

"Yes," he said. "The police picked him up in a Vermont hotel last night. They're bringing him back here this morning."

"What will he be charged with?"

"Complicity in a blackmail scheme," Stan said.

"Blackmail?"

Stan nodded. "I'll be able to tell you more when he's here and questioned. By the time I come to take you to Helen's, it should all be pretty well out in the open."

"Must I wait until then?"

"I'm afraid so," he said. "The nurse will get you dressed and I'll come for you shortly after four."

She was feeling so well she was able to dress herself and pack her small bag. Then she waited for Stan to come. But when the door of the hospital room opened she received a disappointment. It was not Stan who came in but his brother, Alex.

Alex looked more sober than usual. There was little of his usual mockery about him. He said, "I see you've been waiting for me."

She stood up. "Waiting for Stan," she said.

"Of course."

"Where is he?" she asked nervously.

"Kept away on police business," Alex said.

Her eyes widened. "What sort of police business?"

"Nothing for you to worry about. It has to do with Mother's death and the death of that girl, Rosalie. Also Harvey Richard is being questioned."

"Stan said that he would be."

Alex picked up her bag. "So I've been delegated to take you to Helen's."

"Thanks. How is your father?"

"Home," Alex said. "He's feeling very badly about Mother's death. At his age it will take him some time to completely recover from it."

"I realize that," she said.

Alex gave her a grim look. "You see what I meant when I

warned you not to marry in with the Moores."

"I don't. Not yet. I'm still in the dark about so many things," she told him.

"Wait until you get to Helen's," he said. "I expect that Stan will meet us there as soon as he's free."

Alex carried her bag in one hand and used the other to help her down the hospital steps and over to his car in the crowded parking lot. He opened the door for her and when she was safely in the front seat he got in beside her and started the car.

As they drove out onto the street, she said, "Has there been much about this in the papers? I haven't seen any yet."

"I'm afraid so," the young man with the horn-rimmed glasses said grimly. "It makes a pretty sensational case."

"That's too bad."

"Mother wouldn't have liked it. She always was so anxious to avoid any scandal," Alex said.

"Is she mentioned a lot?"

"They've even used her photo."

"I see," she said with a sigh.

"Well, it will be bad for a little while and then people may forget," Alex said.

"They're bound to."

"I'm worried most about my father," Alex said.

"Naturally."

They reached Helen's place and went inside. The pretty dark girl tearfully greeted Beth and held her close to her for a long moment.

"Poor dear Beth," she said.

"Has Stan gotten back yet?" Beth asked.

"Not yet," her sister-in-law said. "He should be here soon. Meanwhile I'll show you to your room."

This took some time and when they returned to the living

room Ted Allan was standing there with Alex. Helen's husband looked rather shame-faced.

"Sorry to have been the cause of so much trouble for you, Beth," he apologized.

She managed a wan smile for him. "Sometimes this kind of trouble is hard to avoid."

Helen looked uneasy. "I wonder what is keeping Stan."

Alex said, "He'll be here soon." And he led Beth to an easy chair. "You're just out of the hospital. Don't make it harder than you have to on yourself."

"Thanks," she said, settling in the chair. But she was more nervous than weak. She asked them, "Aren't any of you going to tell me anything?"

"Not much to tell until Stan gets here," Alex said.

"Can I see some of the newspapers?" she asked.

"Later," Helen said. "I think you really should hear it all from Stan first."

"I know about Rosalie," Beth said. "She was the ghost."

"Not hard for her," Alex said bitterly. "She looked exactly like Jean and it seems Jean had given her a key to your place."

"I knew somebody must have one," Beth said.

At this point the front door opened and Stan came in. He nodded wearily to them all and went straight over to Beth and kissed her on the temple.

"Sorry I couldn't make it at the hospital," he said.

"It doesn't matter," she told him. "I'm almost sick with suspense. Tell me what is happening and what has happened. I only know such a small part of it."

Stan took a position in the middle of the room with the others at various points around him. He said, "I suppose I'd better go back to the night of the storm. When you had your fever collapse."

"Go on," she said.

Stan gave her a serious look. "Jean came running into the room and I followed her. We quarreled and then you collapsed. She left as I tended to you. She went back to the house and then over to Harvey Richard's cottage. In the meanwhile, the family returned home and the ambulance came for you. Father went with you to the hospital."

"I remember," she said.

"In the meantime Mother separated from the group and drove to my place. She knew Jean had gone there and she wanted to reason with her. To plead with her not to disgrace the family. She reached the house and Jean was not there. Then my mother crossed the lawn in the storm to look into the windows of the Richard cottage. She saw Jean in his arms. She waited and when Jean left the cottage she accosted her and there was a bitter quarrel between them."

"This was during the time you were placing me in the ambulance?" she said.

"Yes," Stan agreed. "Jean broke away from my mother and went toward the cliff path. She was starting back to the Richard cottage. My mother followed her and there was a struggle in which by a quirk my mother was able to send Jean plunging down over the cliff to her death."

Beth gasped. "So that was it!"

"Yes," Stan said. "Harvey Richard had come out in time to see the climax of the struggle and my mother murdering Jean. He told my mother to drive home and pretend not to worry. To pretend nothing had happened. He would keep silent about it all for a price!"

"Blackmail!" Beth said.

"Nothing less," Stan said grimly. "But he realized that the accident had unhinged my mother's mind before any of the rest of us guessed. He knew that from the moment of Jean's murder my mother was mentally upset. And to be sure she paid him his blackmail money, he brought Rosalie back here and had her play the ghost. A trick to prey on my mother's sick mind. It worked well enough. My mother was paying him regularly and gradually losing her grip on sanity."

Alex spoke up in a harsh tone. "But she wasn't too mad to write down a confession of her crime or of Richard's blackmailing. We even have a record of the checks she cashed to pay him, documented with dates by her."

"We all were afraid Mother was involved in Jean's death," Helen explained. "That is why we tried to keep all the facts we could from you. It wasn't Stan we were protecting, it was Mother. Though even then we weren't certain about whether she'd killed Jean or not."

Stan said, "You know the climax. You were part of it the other night. Rosalie played the ghost in our place and also wrecked that room to upset you. It was their way of getting revenge on me. But she and Harvey Richard forgot that Mother was a madwoman. In the end Mother struck her down and tried to kill you. Thank Heaven you escaped."

Helen said apologetically, "We all owe you a debt. We placed your life in danger to try to save Mother. Try to forgive us."

Alex said, "I was the only one who warned you. Remember?"

"I do," she said. "It's all right. It's over. I'm only sorry it had to end this way. I hope Harvey Richard pays for his crime in full."

"He will," Stan promised. "The evidence is strong against him."

Much later Beth and Stan strolled out to the verandah of Helen's house where they could be alone. She stared out at the ocean and then turned to him and said, "What about the house?"

He smiled. "The things are being moved now. You'll never see it again. Father has invited us to live with him and I've accepted at least for a time."

"I'd like that," she said. "It's a lovely old house."

Stan nodded and took her in his arms. "And it has so many memories for us."

She smiled up at him. "I'm thinking more of the future we'll have there." And their lips met.